HELEN'S BABIES

by
JOHN HABBERTON

Dedication

Everyone knows that there are, in the World, hundreds of thousands of fathers and mothers, each one of whom possesses the best children that ever lived. I am, therefore, moved by a sense of the eternal fitness of things to dedicate this little volume to

The Parents of the
Best Children in the World

with the reminder that it is considered the proper thing for each person, to whom a book is dedicated, to purchase and read a copy.

he first cause, so far as it can be determined, of the existence of this book may be found in the following letter, written by my only married sister, and received by me, Harry Burton, salesman of white goods, bachelor, aged twenty-eight, and received just as I was trying to decide where I should spend a fortnight's vacation:

"Hillcrest, June 15, 1875.

Dear Harry:—Remembering that you are always complaining that you never have a chance to read, and knowing you won't get it this summer, if you spend your vacation among people of your own set, I write to ask you to come up here. I admit that I am not wholly disinterested in inviting you. The truth is, Tom and I are invited to spend a fortnight with my old school-mate, Alice Wayne, who, you know, is the dearest girl in the world, though you didn't obey me and marry her before Frank Wayne appeared. Well, we're dying to go, for Alice and Frank live in splendid style; but as they haven't included our children in their invitation, and have no children of their own, we must leave Budge and Toddie at home. I've no doubt they'll be perfectly safe, for my girl is a jewel, and devoted to the children, but I would feel a great deal easier if there was a man in the house. Besides, there's the silver, and burglars are less likely to break into a house where there's a savage-looking man. (Never mind about thanking me for the compliment.) If you'll only come up, my mind will be completely at rest. The children won't give you the slightest trouble; they're the best children in the world—everybody says so.

"Tom has plenty of cigars, I know, for the money I should have had for a new suit went to pay his cigar-man. He has some new claret, too, that he goes into ecstasies over, though I can't tell it from the vilest black ink, except by the color. Our horses are in splendid condition, and so is the garden—you see I don't forget your old passion for flowers. And, last and best, there never were so many handsome girls at Hillcrest as there are among the summer boarders already here; the girls you are already acquainted with here will see that you meet all the newer acquisitions.

"Reply by telegraph right away. Of course you'll say 'Yes.'

"In great haste, your loving

"Sister Helen.

"P.S.—You shall have our own chamber; it catches every breeze, and commands the finest views. The children's room communicates with it; so, if anything should happen to the darlings at night, you'll be sure to hear them."

"Just the thing!" I ejaculated. Five minutes later I had telegraphed Helen my acceptance of her invitation, and had mentally selected books enough to busy me during a dozen vacations. Without sharing Helen's belief that her boys were the best ones in the world, I knew them well enough to feel assured that they would not give me any annoyance. There were two of them, since Baby Phil died last fall; Budge, the elder, was five years of age, and had generally, during my flying visits to Helen, worn a shy, serious, meditative, noble face, with great, pure, penetrating eyes, that made me almost fear their stare. Tom declared he was a born philanthropist or prophet, and Helen made so free with Miss Mulock's lines as to sing:

"Ah, the day that thou goest a wooing,
Budgie, my boy!"
Toddie had seen but three summers, and was a happy little know-nothing, with a head full of tangled yellow hair, and a very pretty fancy for finding out sunbeams and dancing in them. I had long envied Tom his horses, his garden, his house and his location, and the idea of controlling them for a fortnight was particularly delightful. Tom's taste in cigars and claret I had always respected, while the lady inhabitants of Hillcrest were, according to my memory, much like those of every other suburban village—the fairest of their sex.

Three days later I made the hour and a half trip between New York and Hillcrest, and hired a hackman to drive me over to Tom's. Half a mile from my brother-in-law's residence, our horses shied violently, and the driver, after talking freely to them, turned to me and remarked:

"That was one of the 'Imps.'"

"What was?" I asked.

"WE CALL 'EM THE IMPS"
"That little cuss that scared the hosses. There he is, now, holdin' up that piece of brushwood. 'Twould be just like his cheek, now, to ask me to let him ride. Here he comes, runnin'. Wonder where t'other is?—they most generally travel together. We call 'em the Imps, about these parts, because they're so uncommon likely at mischief. Always skeerin' hosses, or chasin' cows, or frightenin' chickens. Nice enough father an' mother, too— queer, how young ones do turn out!"

As he spoke, the offending youth came panting beside our carriage, and in a very dirty sailor-suit, and under a broad-brimmed straw hat, with one stocking about his ankle, and two shoes averaging about two buttons each, I recognized my nephew, Budge! About the same time there emerged from the bushes by the roadside a smaller boy, in a green gingham dress, a ruffle which might once have been white, dirty stockings, blue slippers worn through at the toes, and an old-fashioned straw turban. Thrusting into the dust of

2

the road a branch from a bush, and shouting, "Here's my grass-cutter!" he ran toward us enveloped in a "pillar of cloud," which might have served the purpose of Israel in Egypt. When we paused, and the dust had somewhat subsided, I beheld the unmistakable lineaments of the child Toddie!

"They're—my nephews," I gasped.

"What!" exclaimed the driver. "By gracious! I forgot you were going to Colonel Lawrence's! I didn't tell anything but the truth about 'em, though; they're smart enough, an' good enough, as boys go; but they'd never die of the complaint that children has in Sunday-school books."

"Budge," said I, with all the sternness I could command, "do you know me?"

The searching eyes of the embryo prophet and philanthropist scanned me for a moment, then their owner replied:

"Yes, you're Uncle Harry. Did you bring us anything?"

"Bring us anything?" echoed Toddie.

"I wish I could have brought you some big whippings," said I, with great severity of manner, "for behaving so badly. Get into this carriage."

"Come on, Tod," shouted Budge, although Toddie's farther ear was not a yard from Budge's mouth, "Uncle Harry's going to take us riding!"

"HERE'S MY GRASS-CUTTER"
"Going to take us riding!" echoed Toddie, with the air of one in a reverie; both the echo and the reverie I soon learned were characteristics of Toddie.

As they clambered into the carriage I noticed that each one carried a very dirty towel, knotted in the center into what is known as a slip-noose knot, drawn very tight. After some moments of disgusted contemplation of these rags, without being in the least able to comprehend their purpose, I asked Budge what those towels were for.

"They're not towels—they're dollies," promptly answered my nephew.

"Goodness!" I exclaimed. "I should think your mother could buy you respectable dolls, and not let you appear in public with those loathsome rags."

"We don't like buyed dollies," explained Budge. "These dollies is lovely; mine's name is Mary, an' Toddie's is Marfa."

"Marfa?" I queried.

"Yes; don't you know about

'Marfa and Mary's jus' gone along
To ring dem charmin' bells,'
that them Jubilees sings about?"

"Oh, Martha, you mean?"

"Yes, Marfa—that's what I say. Toddie's dolly's got brown eyes, an' my dolly's got blue eyes."

"I want to shee yours watch," remarked Toddie, snatching at my chain, and rolling into my lap.

"Oh—oo—ee, so do I," shouted Budge, hastening to occupy one knee, and in transitu wiping his shoes on my trousers and the skirts of my coat. Each imp put an arm about me to steady himself, as I produced my three-hundred dollar time-keeper, and showed them the dial.

"I want to see the wheels go round," said Budge.

"Want to shee wheels go wound," echoed Toddie.

"No; I can't open my watch where there's so much dust," I said.

"What for?" inquired Budge.

"Want to shee the wheels go wound," repeated Toddie.

"The dust gets inside the watch and spoils it," I explained.

"Want to shee the wheels go wound," said Toddie, once more.

"I tell you I can't, Toddie," said I, with considerable asperity. "Dust spoils watches."

The innocent gray eyes looked up wonderingly, the dirty but pretty lips parted slightly, and Toddie murmured:—

"Want to shee the wheels go wound."

I abruptly closed my watch, and put it into my pocket. Instantly Toddie's lower lip commenced to turn outward, and continued to do so, until I seriously feared the bony portion of his chin would be exposed to view. Then his lower jaw dropped, and he cried:—

"Ah—h—h—h—h—h—want—to—shee—the wheels—go wou—ound."

"Charles" (Charles is his baptismal name),—"Charles," I exclaimed, with some anger, "stop that noise this instant! Do you hear me?"

4

"Yes—oo—oo—oo—ahoo—ahoo."

"Then stop it."

"Wants to shee——"

"Toddie, I've got some candy in my trunk, but I won't give you a bit if you don't stop that infernal noise."

"Well, I wants to shee wheels go wound. Ah—ah—h—h—h—h!"

"Toddie, dear, don't cry so. Here's some ladies coming in a carriage; you wouldn't let them see you crying, would you? You shall see the wheels go round as soon as we get home."

"WHEELS GO WOUND"

A carriage containing a couple of ladies was rapidly approaching, as Toddie again raised his voice.

"Ah—h—h—want's to shee wheels——"

Madly I snatched my watch from my pocket, opened the case, and exposed the works to view. The other carriage was passing ours, and I dropped my head to avoid meeting the glance of the unknown occupants, for my few moments of contact with my dreadful nephews had made me feel inexpressibly unneat. Suddenly the carriage with the ladies stopped. I heard my own name spoken, and, raising my head quickly (encountering Budge's bullet head en route, to the serious disarrangement of my hat), I looked into the other carriage. There, erect, fresh, neat, composed, bright-eyed, fair-faced, smiling and observant,—she would have been all this, even if the angel of the resurrection had just sounded his dreadful trump,—sat Miss Alice Mayton, a lady who, for about a year, I had been adoring from afar.

"When did you arrive, Mr. Burton?" she asked, "and how long have you been officiating as child's companion? You're certainly a happy-looking trio—so unconventional. I hate to see children all dressed up and stiff as little manikins, when they go out to ride. And you look as if you'd been having such a good time with them."

"I—I assure you, Miss Mayton," said I, "that my experience has been the exact reverse of a pleasant one. If King Herod were yet alive I'd volunteer as an executioner, and engage to deliver two interesting corpses at a moment's notice."

"You dreadful wretch!" exclaimed the lady. "Mother, let me make you acquainted with Mr. Burton, Helen Lawrence's brother. How is your sister, Mr. Burton?"

5

"I don't know," I replied; "she has gone with her husband on a fortnight's visit to Captain and Mrs. Wayne, and I've been silly enough to promise to have an eye to the place while they're away."

"Why, how delightful!" exclaimed Miss Mayton. "Such horses! Such flowers! Such a cook!"

"And such children," said I, glaring suggestively at the imps, and rescuing from Toddie a handkerchief which he had extracted from my pocket, and was waving to the breeze.

"Why, they're the best children in the world. Helen told me so the first time I met her this season. Children will be children, you know. We had three little cousins with us last summer, and I'm sure they made me look years older than I really am."

"How young you must be, then, Miss Mayton!" said I. I suppose I looked at her as if I meant what I said, for although she inclined her head and said, "Oh, thank you," she didn't seem to turn my compliment off in her usual invulnerable style. Nothing happening in the course of conversation ever discomposed Alice Mayton for more than a hundred seconds, however, so she soon recovered her usual expression and self-command, as her next remark fully indicated.

"I believe you arranged the floral decorations at the St. Zephaniah's Fair, last winter, Mr. Burton? 'Twas the most tasteful display of the season. I don't wish to give any hints, but at Mrs. Clarkson's, where we're boarding, there's not a flower in the whole garden. I break the Tenth Commandment dreadfully every time I pass Colonel Lawrence's garden. Good-by, Mr. Burton."

"I BELIEVE YOU ARRANGED THE FLORAL DECORATIONS"
"Ah, thank you; I shall be delighted. Good-by."

"Of course you'll call," said Miss Mayton, as her carriage started. "It's dreadfully stupid here—no men except on Sundays."

I bowed assent. In the contemplation of all the shy possibilities which my short chat with Miss Mayton had suggested, I had quite forgotten my dusty clothing and the two living causes thereof. While in Miss Mayton's presence the imps had preserved perfect silence, but now their tongues were loosened.

"Uncle Harry," said Budge, "do you know how to make whistles?"

"Unken Hawwy," murmured Toddie, "does you love dat lady?"

"No, Toddie, of course not."

"Then you's a baddy man, an' de Lord won't let you go to heaven if you don't love peoples."

6

"Yes, Budge," I answered hastily, "I do know how to make whistles, and you shall have one."

"Lord don't like mans what don't love peoples," reiterated Toddie.

"All right, Toddie," said I. "I'll see if I can't please the Lord some way. Driver, whip up, won't you? I'm in a hurry to turn these youngsters over to the girl, and ask her to drop them into the bath-tub."

DROPPING THEM INTO THE BATHTUB

I found Helen had made every possible arrangement for my comfort. Her room commanded exquisite views of mountain slope and valley, and even the fact that the imps' bedroom adjoined mine gave me comfort, for I thought of the pleasure of contemplating them while they were asleep, and beyond the power of tormenting their deluded uncle.

At the supper-table Budge and Toddie appeared cleanly clothed and in their rightful faces. Budge seated himself at the table; Toddie pushed back his high-chair, climbed into it, and shouted:—

"Put my legs under ze tabo!"

Rightfully construing this remark as a request to be moved to the table, I fulfilled his desire. The girl poured tea for me and milk for the children, and retired; and then I remembered, to my dismay, that Helen never had a servant in the dining-room, except upon grand occasions, her idea being that servants retail to their friends the cream of the private conversation of the family circle. In principle I agreed with her, but the penalty of the practical application, with these two little cormorants on my hands, was greater suffering than any I had ever been called upon to endure for principle's sake; but there was no help for it. I resignedly rapped on the table, bowed my head, said, "For what we are about to receive, the Lord make us thankful," and asked Budge whether he ate bread or biscuit.

"Why, we ain't asked no blessin' yet," said he.

"Yes, I did, Budge," said I. "Didn't you hear me?"

"Do you mean what you said just now?"

"Yes."

"Oh, I don't think that was no blessin' at all. Papa never says that kind of a blessin'."

"What does papa say, may I ask?" I inquired, with becoming meekness.

7

"Why, papa says, 'Our Father, we thank thee for this food; mercifully remember with us all the hungry and needy to-day, for Christ's sake, Amen.' That's what he says."

"It means the same thing, Budge."

"I don't think it does; and Toddie didn't have no time to say his blessin'. I don't think the Lord'll like it if you do it that way."

"Yes, He will, old boy; He knows what people mean."

"Well, how can he tell what Toddie means if Toddie can't say anything?"

"Wantsh to shay my blessin'," whined Toddie.

It was enough; my single encounter with Toddie had taught me to respect the young gentleman's force of character. So again I bowed my head and repeated what Budge had reported as "papa's blessin'," Budge kindly prompting me where my memory failed. The moment I began, Toddie commenced to jabber rapidly and aloud, and the instant the "Amen" was pronounced he raised his head and remarked with evident satisfaction:—

"I shed my blessin' two timesh."

And Budge said gravely: "Now I guess we're all right."

The supper was an exquisite one, but the appetites of those dreadful children effectually prevented my enjoying the repast. I hastily retired, called the girl, and instructed her to see that the children had enough to eat, and were put to bed immediately after; then I lit a cigar and strolled into the garden. The roses were just in bloom, the air was full of the perfume of honeysuckles, the rhododendrons had not disappeared, while I saw promise of the early unfolding of many other pet flowers of mine. I confess that I took a careful survey of the garden to see how fine a bouquet I might make for Miss Mayton, and was so abundantly satisfied with the material before me that I longed to begin the work at once, but that it would seem too hasty for true gentility. So I paced the paths, my hands behind my back, and my face well hidden by fragrant clouds of smoke, and went into wondering and reveries. I wondered if there was any sense in the language of flowers, of which I had occasionally seen mention made by silly writers; I wished I had learned it if it had any meaning; I wondered if Miss Mayton understood it. At any rate, I fancied I could arrange flowers to the taste of any lady whose face I had ever seen; and for Alice Mayton I would make something so superb that her face could not help lighting up when she beheld it. I imagined just how her bluish-gray eyes would brighten, her cheeks would redden,—not with sentiment, not a bit of it, but with genuine pleasure,— how her strong lips would part slightly and disclose sweet lines not displayed when she held her features well in hand. I—I, a clear-headed, driving, successful salesman of white goods—actually wished I might be divested of all nineteenth-century abilities and characteristics, and be one of those fairies that only silly girls and crazy poets think of, and might, unseen, behold the meeting of my flowers with this highly cultivated specimen of the only sort of flowers our cities produce. What flower did she most resemble? A lily?— no; too—not exactly too bold, but too—too, well, I couldn't think of the word, but clearly it wasn't bold. A rose? Certainly, not like those glorious but blazing remontants,

8

nor yet like the shy, delicate, ethereal tea roses with their tender suggestions of color. Like this perfect Gloire de Dijon, perhaps; strong, vigorous, self-asserting, among its more delicate sisterhood; yet shapely, perfect in outline and development, exquisite, enchanting in its never fully analyzed tints, yet compelling the admiration of everyone, and recalling its admirers again and again by the unspoken appeal of its own perfection—its unvarying radiance.

"Ah—h—h—h—ee—ee—ee—ee—ee—oo —oo—oo—oo!" came from the window over my head. Then came a shout of—"Uncle Harry!" in a voice I recognized as that of Budge. I made no reply: there are moments when the soul is full of utterances unfit to be heard by childish ears. "Uncle Harray!" repeated Budge. Then I heard a window blind open, and Budge exclaiming:—

"Uncle Harry, we want you to come and tell us stories."

I turned my eyes upward quickly, and was about to send a savage negative in the same direction, when I saw in the window a face unknown and yet remembered. Could those great, wistful eyes, that angelic mouth, that spiritual expression, belong to my nephew Budge? Yes, it must be certainly that super-celestial nose and those enormous ears never belonged to anyone else. I turned abruptly, and entered the house, and was received at the head of the stairway by two little figures in white, the larger of which remarked:—

"We want you to tell us stories—papa always does nights."

"Very well, jump into bed—what kind of stories do you like?"

"Oh, 'bout Jonah," said Budge.

"'Bout Jonah," echoed Toddie.

"Well, Jonah was out in the sun one day, and a gourd-vine grew up all of a sudden, and made it nice and shady for him, and then it all faded as quick as it came."

A dead silence prevailed for a moment, and then Budge indignantly remarked:

"That ain't Jonah a bit—I know 'bout Jonah."

"Oh, you do, do you?" said I. "Then maybe you'll be so good as to enlighten me?"

"Huh?"

"If you know about Jonah, tell me the story; I'd really enjoy listening to it."

"Well," said Budge, "Once upon a time the Lord told Jonah to go to Nineveh and tell the people they was all bad. But Jonah didn't want to go, so he went on a boat that was going to Joppa. An' then there was a big storm, an' it rained an' blowed and the big waves went as high as a house. An' the sailors thought there must be somebody on the

9

boat that the Lord didn't like. An' Jonah said he guessed he was the man. So they picked him up and froed him in the ocean, an' I don't think it was well for 'em to do that after Jonah told the troof. An' a big whale was comin' along, an' he was awful hungry, 'cos the little fishes what he likes to eat all went down to the bottom of the ocean when it began to storm, and whales can't go to the bottom of the ocean, 'cos they have to come up to breeve, an' little fishes don't. An' Jonah found 'twas all dark inside the whale, and there wasn't any fire there, an' it was all wet, an' he couldn't take off his clothes to dry, 'cos there wasn't no place to hang 'em, and there wasn't no windows to look out of, nor nothin' to eat, nor nothin' nor nothin' nor nothin'. So he asked the Lord to let him out, an' the Lord was sorry for him, an' He made the whale go up close to the land, an' Jonah jumped right out of his mouth, and wasn't he glad? An' then he went to Nineveh, an' done what the Lord told him to, an' he ought to have done it in the first place if he had known what was good for him."

BUDGE'S IDEA OF JONAH AND THE WHALE

"Done first payshe, know what's dood for him," asserted Toddie, in support of his brother's assertion. "Tell us 'nudder story."

"Oh, no, sing us a song," suggested Budge.

"Shing us shong," echoed Toddie.

I searched my mind for a song, but the only one which came promptly was "M'Appari," several bars of which I gave my juvenile audience, when Budge interrupted me, saying:—

"I don't think that's a very good song."

"Why not, Budge?"

"'Cos I don't. I don't know a word what you're talking 'bout."

"Shing 'bout 'Glory, glory, hallelulyah,'" suggested Toddie, and I meekly obeyed. The old air has a wonderful influence over me. I heard it in western campmeetings and negro cabins when I was a boy; I saw the 22nd Massachusetts march down Broadway, singing the same air during the rush to the front in the early days of the war; I have heard it sung by warrior tongues in nearly every southern state; I heard it roared by three hundred good old Hunker Democrats as they escorted New York's first colored regiment to their place of embarkation; my old brigade sang it softly, but with a swing that was terrible in its earnestness, as they lay behind their stacks of arms just before going into action; I have heard it played over the grave of many a dead comrade; the semi-mutinous—th cavalry became peaceful and patriotic again, as their bandmaster played the old air after having asked permission to try his hand on them; it is the same that burst forth spontaneously in our barracks, on that glorious morning when we learned that the war was over, and it was sung, with words adapted to the occasion, by some good rebel friends of mine, on our first social meeting after the war. All these recollections came hurrying into my mind as I sang, and probably excited me beyond my knowledge. For Budge suddenly remarked:—

"Don't sing that all day, Uncle Harry; you sing so loud, it hurts my head."

"Beg your pardon, Budge," said I. "Good night."

"Why, Uncle Harry, are you going? You didn't hear us say our prayers,—papa always does."

"Oh! Well, go ahead."

"You must say yours first," said Budge; "that's the way papa does."

"Very well," said I, and I repeated St. Chrysostom's prayer, from the Episcopal service. I had hardly said "Amen," when Budge remarked:—

"My papa don't say any of them things at all; I don't think that's a very good prayer."

"Well, you say a good prayer, Budge."

"WE HOPE HE'S GOT LOTS OF CANDY"

"All right." Budge shut his eyes, dropped his voice to the most perfect tone of supplication, while his face seemed fit for a sleeping angel; then he said:—

"Dear Lord, we thank you for lettin' us have a good time to-day, an' we hope all the little boys everywhere have had good times too. We pray you to take care of us an' everybody else to-night, an' don't let 'em have any trouble. Oh, yes, an' Uncle Harry's got some candy in his trunk, 'cos he said so in the carriage,—we thank you for lettin' Uncle Harry come to see us, an' we hope he's got lots of candy—lots an' piles. An' we pray you to take care of all the poor little boys and girls that haven't got any papas an' mammas an' Uncle Harrys an' candy an' beds to sleep in. An' take us all to Heaven when we die, for Christ's sake. Amen. Now give us the candy, Uncle Harry."

"Hush, Budge; don't Toddie say any prayers?"

"Oh, yes; go on, Tod."

Toddie closed his eyes, wriggled, twisted, breathed hard and quick, acting generally as if prayers were principally a matter of physical exertion. At last he began:—

"Dee Lord, not make me sho bad, an' besh mamma, an' papa, an' Budgie, an' doppity,[1] an' both boggies,[2] an' all good people in dish house, an' everybody else, an' my dolly. A—a—amen!"

[1] Grandfather.

[2] Grandmothers.

"Now give us the candy," said Budge, with the usual echo from Toddie.

11

I hastily extracted the candy from my trunk, gave some to each boy, the recipients fairly shrieking with delight, and once more said good night.

"Oh, you didn't give us any pennies," said Budge. "Papa gives us some to put in our banks, every night."

"Well, I haven't got any now—wait until to-morrow."

"Then we want drinks."

"I'll let Maggie bring you drink."

"Want my dolly," murmured Toddie.

I found the knotted towels, took the dirty things up gingerly and threw them upon the bed.

"Now want to shee wheels go wound," said Toddie.

I hurried out of the room and slammed the door. I looked at my watch—it was half-past eight; I had spent an hour and a half with those dreadful children. They were funny, to be sure—I found myself laughing, in spite of my indignation. Still, if they were to monopolize my time as they had already done, when was I to do my reading? Taking Fiske's "Cosmic Philosophy" from my trunk, I descended to the back parlor, lit a cigar and a student-lamp, and began to read. I had not fairly commenced when I heard a patter of small feet, and saw my elder nephew before me. There was sorrowful protestation in every line of his countenance, as he exclaimed:—

"You didn't say 'Good-by,' nor 'God bless you,' nor anything."

"Oh—good-by."

"Good-by."

"God bless you."

"God bless you."

Budge seemed waiting for something else. At last he said:—

"Papa says, 'God bless everybody.'"

"Well, God bless everybody."

"God bless everybody," responded Budge, and turned silently and went upstairs.

"Bless your tormenting honest little heart." I said to myself; "if men trusted God as you do your papa, how little business there'd be for preachers to do."

12

The night was a perfect one. The pure, fresh air, the perfume of the flowers, the music of the insect choir in the trees and shrubbery—the very season itself seemed to forbid my reading philosophy, so I laid Fiske aside, delighted myself with a few rare bits from Paul Hayne's new volume of poems, read a few chapters of "One Summer," and finally sauntered off to bed. My nephews were slumbering sweetly; it seemed impossible that the pure, exquisite, angelic faces before me belonged to my tormentors of a few hours before. As I lay on my couch I could see the dark shadow and rugged crest of the mountain; above it, the silver stars against the blue, and below it the rival lights of the fireflies against the dark background formed by the mountain itself. No rumbling of wheels tormented me, nor any of the thousand noises that fill city air with the spirit of unrest, and I fell into a wonder almost indignant that sensible, comfort-loving beings could live in horrible New York, while such delightful rural homes were so near at hand. Then Alice Mayton came into my mind, and then a customer; later, stars and trade-marks, and bouquets, and dirty nephews, and fireflies and bad accounts, and railway tickets, and candy and Herbert Spencer, mixed themselves confusingly in my mind. Then a vision of a proud angel, in the most fashionable attire and a modern carriage, came and banished them all by its perfect radiance, and I was sinking in the most blissful unconsciousness—

"Ah—h—h—h—h—h—oo—oo—oo—oo—ee—ee—e—"

"Sh—h—h!" I hissed.

The warning was heeded, and I soon relapsed into oblivion.

"Ah—h—h—h—oo—oo—ee—ee—EE—ee!"

"Toddie, do you want your uncle to whip you?"

"No."

"Then lie still."

"Well, I'ze lost my dolly, an' I tan't find her anywhere."

"Well, I'll find her for you in the morning."

"Oo—oo—ee—I want my dolly."

"Well, I tell you I'll find her for you in the morning."

"I want her now—oo—oo—"

"You can't have her now, so you can go to sleep."

I ENCOUNTERED A DOOR AJAR
"Oh—oo—oo—oo—ee—"

Springing madly to my feet, I started for the offender's room. I encountered a door ajar by the way, my forehead being the first to discover it. I ground my teeth, lit a candle, and said something—no matter what.

"Oh, you said a bad swear!" ejaculated Toddie; "you won't go to heaven when you die."

"Neither will you, if you howl like a little demon all night. Are you going to be quiet, now?"

"Yesh, but I wants my dolly."

"I don't know where your dolly is—do you suppose I'm going to search this entire house for that confounded dolly?"

"'Tain't 'founded. I wants my dolly."

"I don't know where it is. You don't think I stole your dolly, do you?"

"Well, I wants it, in de bed wif me."

"Charles," said I, "when you arise in the morning, I hope your doll will be found. At present, however, you must be resigned and go to sleep. I'll cover you up nicely"; here I began to rearrange the bed clothing, when the fateful dolly, source of all my woes, tumbled out of them. Toddie clutched it, his whole face lighting up with affectionate delight, and he screamed:—

"Oh, dare is my dee dolly; turn to your own papa, dolly, an' I'll love you."

And that ridiculous child was so completely satisfied by his outlay of affection, that my own indignation gave place to genuine artistic pleasure. One can tire of even beautiful pictures, though, when he is not fully awake, and is holding a candle in a draught of air; so I covered my nephews and returned to my own room, where I mused upon the contradictoriness of childhood until I fell asleep.

THE DOLLY FOUND

In the morning I was awakened very early by the light streaming in the window, the blinds of which I had left open the night before. The air was alive with bird-song, and the eastern sky was flushed with tints which no painter's canvas ever caught. But ante-sunrise skies and songs are not fit subjects for the continued contemplation of men who read until midnight; so I hastily closed the blinds, drew the shade, dropped the curtains and lay down again, dreamily thanking Heaven that I was to fall asleep to such exquisite music. I am sure that I mentally forgave all my enemies as I dropped off into a most delicious doze, but the sudden realization that a light hand was passing over my cheek roused me to savage anger in an instant. I sprang up, and saw Budge shrink timidly away from my bedside.

14

"I was only lovin' you, 'cos you was good, and brought us candy. Papa lets us love him whenever we want to—every morning he does."

"As early as this?" demanded I.

"Yes, just as soon as we can see, if we want to."

Poor Tom! I never could comprehend why, with a good wife, a comfortable income, and a clear conscience, he need always look thin and worn—worse than he ever did in Virginia woods or Louisiana swamps. But now I knew all. And yet, what could one do? That child's eyes and voice, and his expression, which exceeded in sweetness that of any of the angels I had ever imagined,—that child could coax a man to do more self-forgetting deeds than the shortening of his precious sleeping-hours amounted to. In fact, he was fast divesting me of my rightful sleepiness, so I kissed him and said:—

"Run to bed, now, dear old fellow, and let uncle go to sleep again. After breakfast I'll make you a whistle."

"Oh! will you?" The angel turned into a boy at once.

"Yes; now run along."

"A loud whistle—a real loud one?"

"Yes, but not if you don't go right back to bed."

The sound of little footsteps receded as I turned over and closed my eyes. Speedily the bird-song seemed to grow fainter; my thoughts dropped to pieces; I seemed to be floating on fleecy clouds, in company with hundreds of cherubs with Budge's features and night-drawers—

"Uncle Harry!"

May the Lord forget the prayer I put up just then!

"I'll discipline you, my fine little boy," thought I. "Perhaps, if I let you shriek your abominable little throat hoarse, you'll learn better than to torment your uncle, that was just getting ready to love you dearly."

"Uncle Har—ray!"

"Howl away, you little imp," thought I. "You've got me wide awake, and your lungs may suffer for it." Suddenly I heard, although in sleepy tones, and with a lazy drawl, some words which appalled me. The murmurer was Toddie:—

"Want—shee—wheels—go—wound."

15

"Budge!" I shouted, in the desperation of my dread lest Toddie, too, might wake up, "what do you want?"

"Uncle Harry!"

"WHAT!"

"Uncle Harry, what kind of wood are you going to make the whistle out of?"

"I won't make any at all—I'll cut a big stick and give you a sound whipping with it, for not keeping quiet, as I told you to."

"Why, Uncle Harry, papa don't whip us with sticks—he spanks us."

"PAPA DON'T WHIP US WITH STICKS"

Heavens! Papa! papa! papa! Was I never to have done with this eternal quotation of "papa"? I was horrified to find myself gradually conceiving a dire hatred of my excellent brother-in-law. One thing was certain, at any rate: sleep was no longer possible; so I hastily dressed and went into the garden. Among the beauty and the fragrance of the flowers, and in the delicious morning air, I succeeded in regaining my temper, and was delighted, on answering the breakfast-bell, two hours later, to have Budge accost me with:—

"Why, Uncle Harry, where was you? We looked all over the house for you, and couldn't find a speck of you."

The breakfast was an excellent one. I afterward learned that Helen, dear old girl, had herself prepared a bill of fare for every meal I should take in the house. As the table talk of myself and nephews was not such as could do harm by being repeated, I requested Maggie, the servant, to wait upon the children, and I accompanied my request with a small treasury note. Relieved, thus, of all responsibility for the dreadful appetites of my nephews, I did full justice to the repast, and even regarded with some interest and amusement the industry of Budge and Toddie with their tiny forks and spoons. They ate rapidly for a while, but soon their appetites weakened and their tongues were unloosed.

"Ocken Hawwy," remarked Toddie, "daysh an awfoo funny chunt up 'tairs—awfoo big chunt. I show it you after brepspup."

"Toddie's a silly little boy," said Budge, "he always says brepspup for brekbux."[3]

[3] Breakfast.

"Oh! What does he mean by chunt, Budge?"

"I guess he means trunk," replied my oldest nephew.

Recollections of my childish delight in rummaging an old trunk—it seems a century ago that I did it—caused me to smile sympathetically at Toddie, to his apparent great

16

delight. "How delightful it is to strike a sympathetic chord in child nature," thought I; "how quickly the infant eye comprehends the look which precedes the verbal expression of an idea? Dear Toddie! for years we might sit at one table, careless of each other's words, but the casual mention of one of thy delights has suddenly brought our souls into that sweetest of all human communions—that one which doubtless bound the Master himself to that apostle who was otherwise apparently the weakest among the chosen twelve." "An awfoo funny chunt" seemed to annihilate suddenly all differences of age, condition and experience between the wee boy and myself, and——

A direful thought struck me. I dashed up stairs and into my room. Yes, he did mean my trunk. I could see nothing funny about it—quite the contrary. The bond of sympathy between my nephew and myself was suddenly broken. Looking at the matter from the comparative distance which a few weeks have placed between that day and this, I can see that I was unable to consider the scene before me with a calm and unprejudiced mind. I am now satisfied that the sudden birth and hasty decease of my sympathy with Toddie were striking instances of human inconsistency. My soul had gone out to his because he loved to rummage in trunks, and because I imagined he loved to see the monument of incongruous material which resulted from such an operation; the scene before me showed clearly that I had rightly divined my nephew's nature. And yet my selfish instincts hastened to obscure my soul's vision, and to prevent that joy which should ensue when "faith is lost in full fruition."

AN AMATEUR IN PACKING

My trunk had contained nearly everything, for while a campaigner I had learned to reduce packing to an exact science. Now, had there been an atom of pride in my composition I might have glorified myself, for it certainly seemed as if the heap upon the floor could never have come out of a single trunk. Clearly, Toddie was more of a general connoisseur than an amateur in packing. The method of his work I quickly discerned, and the discovery threw some light upon the size of the heap in front of my trunk. A dress hat and its case, when their natural relationship is dissolved, occupy nearly twice as much space as before, even if the former contains a blacking-box not usually kept in it, and the latter a few cigars soaking in bay rum. The same might be said of a portable dressing-case and its contents, bought for me in Vienna by a brother ex-soldier, and designed by an old Continental campaigner to be perfection itself. The straps which prevented the cover from falling entirely back had been cut, broken or parted in some way, and in its hollow lay my dress-coat, tightly rolled up. Snatching it up with a violent exclamation, and unrolling it, there dropped from it—one of those infernal dolls. At the same time a howl was sounded from the doorway.

"You tookted my dolly out of her cradle—I want to wock[4] my dolly—oo—oo—oo—ee—ee—ee—!"

[4] Rock.

"You young scoundrel!" I screamed—yes, howled, I was so enraged—"I've a great mind to cut your throat this minute. What do you mean by meddling with my trunk?"

17

"I—doe—know." Outward turned Toddie's lower lip; I believe the sight of it would move a Bengal tiger to pity, but no such thought occurred to me just then.

"What made you do it?"

"Be—cause."

"Because what?"

"I—doe—know."

Just then a terrific roar arose from the garden. Looking out, I saw Budge with a bleeding finger upon one hand, and my razor in the other; he afterward explained he had been making a boat, and that the knife was bad to him. To apply adhesive plaster to the cut was the work of but a minute, and I had barely completed this surgical operation when Tom's gardener-coachman appeared, and handed me a letter. It was addressed in Helen's well-known hand, and read as follows (the passages in brackets were my own comments):—

"Bloomdale, June 21, 1875.
"Dear Harry:—I'm very happy in the thought that you are with my darling children, and, although I'm having a lovely time here, I often wish I was with you. [Ump—so do I.] I want you to know the little treasures real well. [Thank you, but I don't think I care to extend the acquaintanceship farther than is absolutely necessary.] It seems to me so unnatural that relatives know so little of those of their own blood, and especially of the innocent little spirits whose existence is almost unheeded. [Not when there's unlocked trunks standing about, sis.]

"Now I want to ask a favor of you. When we were boys and girls at home, you used to talk perfect oceans about physiognomy, and phrenology, and unerring signs of character. I thought it was all nonsense then, but if you believe it now, I wish you'd study the children, and give me your well-considered opinion of them. [Perfect demons, ma'am; imps, rascals, born to be hung—both of them.]

"I can't get over the feeling that dear Budge is born for something grand. [Grand nuisance.] He is sometimes so thoughtful and so absorbed, that I almost fear the result of disturbing him; then, he has that faculty of perseverance which seems to be the only thing some men have lacked to make them great. [He certainly has it; he exemplified it while I was trying to get to sleep this morning.]

"Toddie is going to make a poet or a musician or an artist. [That's so; all abominable scamps take to some artistic pursuit as an excuse for loafing.] His fancies take hold of him very strongly. [They do—they do; "shee wheels go wound," for instance.] He has not Budgie's sublime earnestness, but he doesn't need it; the irresistible force with which he is drawn toward whatever is beautiful compensates for the lack. [Ah—perhaps that explains his operation with my trunk.] But I want your own opinion, for I know you make more careful distinction in character than I do.

18

"Delighting myself with the idea that I deserve most of the credit for the lots of reading you will have done by this time, and hoping I shall soon have a line telling me how my darlings are, I am, as ever,

"Your loving sister,
"Helen."

Seldom have I been so roused by a letter as I was by this one, and never did I promise myself more genuine pleasure in writing a reply. I determined that it should be a masterpiece of analysis and of calm yet forcible expression of opinion.

Upon one step, at any rate, I was positively determined. Calling the girl, I asked her where the key was that locked the door between my room and the children.

"Please, sir, Toddie threw it down the well."

"Is there a locksmith in the village?"

"No, sir; the nearest one is at Paterson."

"Is there a screw-driver in the house?"

"Yes, sir."

"Bring it to me, and tell the coachman to get ready at once to drive me to Paterson."

The screw-driver was brought, and with it I removed the lock, got into the carriage, and told the driver to take me to Paterson by the hill road—one of the most beautiful roads in America.

"Paterson!" exclaimed Budge. "Oh, there's a candy store in that town; come on, Toddie."

"Will you?" thought I, snatching the whip and giving the horses a cut. "Not if I can help it. The idea of having such a drive spoiled by the clatter of such a couple!"

Away went the horses, and up went a piercing shriek and a terrible roar. It seemed that both children must have been mortally hurt, and I looked out hastily, only to see Budge and Toddie running after the carriage, and crying pitifully. It was too pitiful,—I could not have proceeded without them, even if they had been inflicted with smallpox. The driver stopped of his own accord,—he seemed to know the children's ways and their results,—and I helped Budge and Toddie in, meekly hoping that the eye of Providence was upon me, and that so self-sacrificing an act would be duly passed to my credit. As we reached the hill road, my kindness to my nephews seemed to assume greater proportions, for the view before me was inexpressibly beautiful. The air was perfectly clear, and across two score towns I saw the great metropolis itself, the silent city of Greenwood beyond it, the bay, the Narrows, the Sound, the two silvery rivers lying between me and the Palisades, and even, across and to the south of Brooklyn, the ocean itself. Wonderful effects of light and shadow, picturesque masses, composed of detached buildings, so far distant that they seemed huddled together; grim factories turned to beautiful palaces by

19

the dazzling reflection of sunlight from their window-panes; great ships seeming in the distance to be toy boats floating idly;—with no signs of life perceptible, the whole scene recalled the fairy stories read in my youthful days, of enchanted cities, and the illusion was greatly strengthened by the dragon-like shape of the roof of New York's new post-office, lying in the center of everything, and seeming to brood over all.

"Uncle Harry!"

Ah, that was what I expected!

"Uncle Harry!"

"Well, Budge?"

"I always think that looks like heaven."

"What does?"

"Why, all that,—from here over to that other sky 'way back there behind everything I mean. And I think that (here he pointed toward what probably was a photographer's roof-light)—that place where it's so shiny, is where God stays."

Bless the child! The scene had suggested only elfindom to me, and yet I prided myself on my quick sense of artistic effects.

"An' over there where that awful bright little speck is," continued Budge, "that's where dear little brother Phillie is; whenever I look over there, I see him putting his hand out."

"Dee 'ittle Phillie went to s'eep in a box, and ze Lord took him to heaven," murmured Toddie, putting together all he had seen and heard of death. Then he raised his voice and exclaimed:—

"Ocken Hawwy, you know what Iz'he goin' do when I be's big man? Iz'he goin' to have hosses an' tarridge, an' Iz'he goin' to wide over all ze chees an' all ze houses an' all ze world an' ewyfing. An' whole lots of little birdies is comin' in my tarridge an' sing songs to me, an' you can come too if you want to, an' we'll have ice-cream an' trawberries an' see 'ittle fishes swimmin' down in ze water, an' we'll get a g'eat big house that's all p'itty on the outshide an' all p'itty on the inshide, an' it'll all be ours an' we'll do just ewyfing we want to."

"Toddie, you're an idealist."

"Ain't a 'dealisht."

"Toddie's a goosey-gander," remarked Budge, with great gravity. "Uncle Harry, do you think heaven's as nice as that place over there?"

"Yes, Budge, a great deal nicer."

20

"Then why don't we die an' go there? I don't want to go on livin' forever an' ever. I don't see why we don't die right away; I think we've lived enough of days."

"The Lord wants us to live until we get good and strong and smart, and do a great deal of good before we die, old fellow—that's why we don't die right away."

"Well, I want to see dear little Phillie, an' if the Lord won't let him come down here, I think he might let me die an' go to heaven. Little Phillie always laughed when I jumped for him. Uncle Harry, angels has wings, don't they?"

"Some people think they have, old boy."

"Well, I know they don't, 'cos if Phillie had wings, I know he'd fly right down an' see me. So they don't."

"But maybe he has to go somewhere else, Budge, or maybe he comes and you can't see him. We can't see angels with our eyes, you know."

"Then what made the Hebrew children in the fiery furnace see one? Their eyes was just like ours, wasn't they? I don't care; I want to see dear little Phillie awful much. Uncle Harry, if I went to heaven, do you know what I'd do?"

"What would you do, Budge?"

"Why, after I saw little Phillie, I'd go right up to the Lord an' give him a great big hug."

"What for, Budge?"

"Oh, 'cos he lets us have nice times, an' gave me my mamma an' papa, an' Phillie—but he took him away again—an' Toddie, but Toddie's a dreadful bad boy sometimes, though."

"Very true, Budge," said I, remembering my trunk and the object of my ride.

"Uncle Harry, did you ever see the Lord?"

"No, Budge; he has been very close to me a good many times, but I never saw him."

"Well, I have; I see him every time I look up in the sky, and there ain't nobody with me."

The driver crossed himself and whispered, "He's foriver a-sayin' that, an' be the powers, I belave him. Sometimes ye'd think that the howly saints themselves was a-spakin' whin that bye gits to goin' on that way."

It was wonderful. Budge's countenance seemed too pure to be of the earth as he continued to express his ideas of the better land and its denizens. As for Toddie, his

21

tongue was going incessantly, although in a tone scarcely audible; but when I chanced to catch his expressions, they were so droll and fanciful, that I took him upon my lap that I might hear him more distinctly. I even detected myself in the act of examining the mental draft of my proposed letter to Helen, and of being ashamed of it. But neither Toddie's fancy nor Budge's spirituality caused me to forget the principal object of my ride. I found a locksmith and left the lock to be fitted with a key; then we drove to the Falls. Both boys discharged volleys of questions as we stood by the gorge, and the fact that the roar of the falling water prevented me from hearing them did not cause them to relax their efforts in the least. I walked to the hotel for a cigar, taking the children with me. I certainly spent no more than three minutes in selecting and lighting a cigar, and asking the barkeeper a few questions about the Falls; but when I turned, the children were missing, nor could I see them in any direction. Suddenly, before my eyes, arose from the nearer brink of the gorge two yellowish disks, which I recognized as the hats of my nephews; then I saw between the disks and me two small figures lying upon the ground. I was afraid to shout, for fear of scaring them if they happened to hear me. I bounded across the grass, industriously raving and praying by turns. They were lying on their stomachs and looking over the edge of the cliff. I approached them on tiptoe, threw myself upon the ground, and grasped a foot of each child.

"Oh, Uncle Harry!" screamed Budge in my ear, as I dragged him close to me, kissing and shaking him alternately; "I hunged over more than Toddie did."

"I HUNGED OVER MORE THAN TODDIE DID"

"Well, I—I—I—I—I—I—I—hunged over a good deal, anyhow," said Toddie, in self-defense.

That afternoon I devoted to making a bouquet for Miss Mayton, and a most delightful occupation I found it. It was no florist's bouquet, composed of only a few kinds of flowers, wired upon sticks, and arranged according to geometric pattern. I used many a rare flower, too shy of bloom to recommend itself to florists; I combined tints almost as numerous as the flowers were, and perfumes to which city bouquets are utter strangers. Arranging flowers is a favorite pastime of mine, but upon this particular occasion I enjoyed my work more than I had ever done before. Not that I was in love with Miss Mayton; a man may honestly and strongly admire a handsome, brilliant woman without being in love with her; he can delight himself in trying to give her pleasure, without feeling it necessary that she shall give him herself in return. Since I arrived at years of discretion I have always smiled sarcastically at the mention of the generosity of men who were in love; they have seemed to me rather to be asking an immense price for what they offered. I had no such feeling toward Miss Mayton. There have been heathens who have offered gifts to goddesses out of pure adoration and without any idea of ever having the exclusive companionship of their favorite divinities. I never offered Miss Mayton any attention which did not put me into closer sympathy with these same great-souled old Pagans; and with such Christians as follow their good example. With each new grace my bouquet took on, my pleasure and satisfaction increased at the thought of how she would enjoy the completed evidence of my taste.

22

At length it was finished, but my delight suddenly became clouded by the dreadful thought, "What will folks say?" Had we been in New York instead of Hillcrest, no one but the florist, his messenger, the lady and myself would know if I sent a bouquet to Miss Mayton; but in Hillcrest, with its several hundred native-born gossips, and its acquaintance of everybody with everybody else and their affairs—I feared talk. Upon the discretion of Mike, the coachman, I could safely rely; I had already confidentially conveyed sundry bits of fractional currency to him, and informed him of one of the parties at our store whose family Mike had known in Old Erin; but every one knew where Mike was employed; every one knew—mysterious, unseen and swift are the ways of communication in the country!—that I was the only gentleman at present residing at Colonel Lawrence's. Ah!—I had it. I had seen in one of the library drawers a small pasteboard box, shaped like a bandbox—doubtless that would hold it. I found the box—it was of just the size I needed. I dropped my card into the bottom—no danger of a lady not finding the card accompanying a gift of flowers—neatly fitted the bouquet in the center of the box, and went in search of Mike. He winked cheeringly as I explained the nature of his errand, and he whispered:—

"I'll do it as clane as a whistle, yer honor. Mistress Clarkson's cook an' mesilf understhand each other, an' I'm used to goin' up the back way. Dhivil a man can see but the angels, an' they won't tell."

"Very well, Mike; here's a dollar for you; you'll find the box on the hat-rack, in the hall."

Half an hour later, while I sat in my chamber window, reading, I beheld Mike, cleanly shaved, dressed and brushed, swinging up the road, with my box balanced on one of his enormous hands. With a head full of pleasing fancies, I went down to supper. My new friends were unusually good. Their ride seemed to have toned down their boisterousness and elevated their little souls; their appetites exhibited no diminution of force, but they talked but little, and all that they said was smart, funny, or startling—so much so that when, after supper, they invited me to put them to bed, I gladly accepted the invitation. Toddie disappeared somewhere, and came back very disconsolate.

"I can't find my dolly's k'adle," he whined.

"Never mind, old pet," said I, soothingly. "Uncle will ride you on his foot."

"But I want my dolly's k'adle," said he, piteously rolling out his lower lip.

I remembered my experience when Toddie wanted to "shee wheels go wound," and I trembled.

"Toddie," said I, in a tone so persuasive that it would be worth thousands a year to me, as a salesman, if I could only command it at will; "Toddie, don't you want to ride on uncle's back?"

"No; want my dolly's k'adle."

"Don't you want me to tell you a story?"

For a moment Toddie's face indicated a terrible internal conflict between old Adam and mother Eve, but curiosity finally overpowered natural depravity, and Toddie murmured:—Yesh."

"What shall I tell you about?"

"'Bout Nawndeark."

"About what?"

"He means Noah an' the ark," exclaimed Budge.

"Datsh what I shay—Nawndeark," declared Toddie.

"Well," said I, hastily refreshing my memory by picking up the Bible,—for Helen, like most people, is pretty sure to forget to pack her Bible when she runs away from home for a few days,—"well, once it rained forty days and nights, and everybody was drowned from the face of the earth excepting Noah, a righteous man, who was saved with all his family, in an ark which the Lord commanded him to build."

"Uncle Harry," said Budge, after contemplating me with open eyes and mouth for at least two minutes after I had finished, "do you think that's Noah?"

"Certainly, Budge; here's the whole story in the Bible."

"Well, I don't think it's Noah one single bit," said he, with increasing emphasis.

"I'm beginning to think we read different Bibles, Budge; but let's hear your version."

"Huh?"

"Tell me about Noah, if you know so much about him."

"I will, if you want me to. Once the Lord felt so uncomfortable 'cos folks was bad that he was sorry he ever made anybody, or any world or anything. But Noah wasn't bad—the Lord liked him first-rate, so he told Noah to build a big ark, and then the Lord would make it rain so everybody should be drownded but Noah an' his little boys an' girls, an' doggies, an' pussies, an' mamma cows, an' little-boy cows, an' little-girl cows, an' hosses, an' everything—they'd go in the ark an' wouldn't get wetted a bit, when it rained. An' Noah took lots of things to eat in the ark—cookies an' milk, an' oatmeal an' strawberries, an' porgies an'—oh, yes; an' plum puddin's an' pumpkin pies. But Noah didn't want everybody to get drownded, so he talked to folks an' said, 'It's goin' to rain awful pretty soon; you'd better be good, an' then the Lord'll let you come into my ark." An' they jus' said 'Oh, if it rains we'll go in the house till it stops'; an' other folks said, 'We ain't afraid of rain—we've got an umbrella.' An' some more said, they wasn't goin' to be afraid of just a rain. But it did rain, though, an' folks went in their houses an' the water came in, an' they got on the tops of the houses, an' up in big trees, an' up in mountains, an' the water went after 'em everywhere an' drownded everybody, only just except Noah and the people in the ark. An' it rained forty days an' nights, an' then it stopped, an' Noah got out of the ark, an' he an' his little boys an' girls went wherever they wanted to, an' everything in the world was all theirs; there wasn't anybody to tell 'em to go home, nor no Kindergarten schools to go to, nor no bad boys to fight 'em, nor nothin'. Now tell us 'nother story."

I determined that I would not again attempt to repeat portions of the Scripture narrative—my experience in that direction had not been encouraging. I ventured upon a war story.

"Do you know what the war was?" I asked, by way of reconnoissance.

"Oh, yes," said Budge, "papa was there an' he's got a sword; don't you see it, hangin' up there?"

"WE'VE GOT AN UMBRELLA"
Yes, I saw it, and the difference between the terrible field where last I saw Tom's sword in action, and this quiet room where it now hung, forced me into a reverie from which I was aroused by Budge remarking:—

"Ain't you goin' to tell us one?"

"Oh, yes, Budge. One day while the war was going on, there was a whole lot of soldiers going along a road, and they were hungry as they could be; they hadn't had anything to eat that day."

"Why didn't they go into the houses, and tell the people they was hungry? That's what I do when I goes along roads."

"Because the people in that country didn't like them; the brothers and papas and husbands of those people were soldiers, too; but they didn't like the soldiers I told you about first, and they wanted to kill them."

"I don't think they were a bit nice," said Budge, with considerable decision.

"Well, the first soldiers wanted to kill them, Budge."

"Then they was all bad, to want to kill each other."

"Oh no, they weren't; there were a great many real good men on both sides."

Poor Budge looked sadly puzzled, as he had an excellent right to do, since the wisest and best men are sorely perplexed by the nature of warlike feeling.

25

"Both parties of soldiers were on horseback," I continued, "and they were near each other, and when they saw each other they made their horses run fast, and the bugles blew, and the soldiers all took their swords out to kill each other with. Just then a little boy, who had been out in the woods to pick berries for his mamma, tried to run across the road, and caught his toe some way, and fell down and cried. Then somebody hallooed 'Halt!' very loud, and all the horses on one side stopped, and then somebody else hallooed 'Halt!' and a lot of bugles blew, and every horse on the other side stopped, and one soldier jumped off his horse, and picked up the little boy—he was only about as big as you, Budge—and tried to comfort him, and then a soldier from the other side came up to look at him; and then more soldiers came from both sides to look at him; and when he got better and walked home, the soldiers all rode away, because they didn't feel like fighting just then."

"O Uncle Harry! I think it was an awful good soldier that got off his horse to take care of that poor little boy."

"Do you, Budge? who do you think it was?"

"I dunno."

"It was your papa."

"Oh—h—h—h!" If Tom could have but seen the expression upon his boy's face as he prolonged this exclamation, his loss of one of the grandest chances a cavalry officer ever had would not have seemed so great to him as it had done for years. He seemed to take in the story in all its bearings, and his great eyes grew in depth as they took on the far-away look which seemed too earnest for the strength of an earthly being to support.

But Toddie—he who a fond mamma thought endowed with art sense—Toddie had throughout my recital the air of a man who was musing on some affair of his own, and Budge's exclamation had hardly died away, when Toddie commenced to weave aloud an extravaganza wholly his own.

"When I was a soldier," he remarked, very gravely, "I had a coat an' a hat on, an' a muff, an' a little knake[5] wound my neck to keep me warm, an' it wained, an' hailed, an' 'tormed, an' I felt bad, so I whallowed a sword an' burned me all down dead."

[5] Snake: tippet.

"And how did you get here?" I asked, with interest proportioned to the importance of Toddie's last clause.

"Oh, I got up from the burn-down dead, an' comed right here. I want my dolly's k'adle."

O persistent little dragon! If you were of age, what a fortune you might make in business!

26

"WHEN I WAS A SOLDIER," REMARKED TODDIE

"Uncle Harry, I wish my papa would come home right away," said Budge.

"Why, Budge?"

"I want to love him for bein' so good to that poor little boy in the war."

"Ocken Hawwy, I wants my dolly's k'adle, 'tause my dolly's in it, an' I want to shee her"; thus spake Toddie.

"Don't you think the Lord loved my papa awful much for doin' that sweet thing, Uncle Harry?" asked Budge.

"Yes, old fellow, I feel sure that he did."

"Lord lovesh my papa vewy much, so I love ze Lord vewy much," remarked Toddie. "An' I wants my dolly's k'adle an' my dolly."

"Toddie, I don't know where either of them are—I can't find them now—do wait until morning, when Uncle Harry will look for them."

"I don't see how the Lord can get along in heaven without my papa, Uncle Harry," said Budge.

"Lord takesh papa to heaven, an' Budge an' me, and we'll go walkin' an' see ze Lord, an play wif ze angels' wings, an hazh good timsh, an' never have to go to bed at all, at all."

Pure-hearted little innocents! compared with older people whom we endure, how great thy faith and how few thy faults! How superior thy love——

A knock at the door interrupted me. "Come in!" I shouted.

In stepped Mike, with an air of the greatest secrecy, handed me a letter and the identical box in which I had sent the flowers to Miss Mayton. What could it mean? I hastily opened the envelope, and at the same time Toddie shrieked:—

"Oh, darsh my dolly's k'adle—dare tizh!" snatched and opened the box, and displayed—his doll! My heart sickened, and did not regain its strength during the perusal of the following note:—

"Miss Mayton herewith returns to Mr. Burton the package which just arrived, with his card. She recognizes the contents as a portion of the apparent property of one of Mr. Burton's nephews, but is unable to understand why it should have been sent to her.

"June 20, 1875."

"Toddie," I roared, as my younger nephew caressed his loathsome doll, and murmured endearing words to it, "where did you get that box?"

"On the hat-wack," replied the youth, with perfect fearlessness. "I keeps it in ze book-case djawer, and somebody took it 'way, and put nasty ole flowers in it."

"Where are those flowers?" I demanded.

Toddie looked up with considerable surprise, but promptly replied:—

"I froed 'em away—don't want no ole flowers in my dolly's k'adle. That's ze way she wocks—see!" And the horrible little destroyer of human hopes rolled that box back and forth with the most utter unconcern, as he spoke endearing words to the substitute for my beautiful bouquet!

To say that I looked at Toddie reprovingly is to express my feelings in the most inadequate language, but of language in which to express my feelings to Toddie, I could find absolutely none. Within two or three short moments I had discovered how very anxious I really was to merit Miss Mayton's regard, and how very different was the regard I wanted from that which I had previously hoped might be accorded me. It seemed too ridiculous to be true that I, who had for years had dozens of charming lady acquaintances, and yet had always maintained my common sense and self-control; I, who had always considered it unmanly for a man to specially interest himself in any lady until he had an income of five thousand a year; I, who had skilfully, and many times, argued that life attachments, or attempts thereat, which were made without a careful preliminary study of the mental characteristics of the partner desired, were the most unpardonable folly,—I had transgressed every one of my own rules, and, as if to mock me for any pretended wisdom and care, my weakness was made known to me by a three-year-old marplot and a hideous rag doll!

That merciful and ennobling dispensation by which Providence enables us to temper the severity of our own sufferings by alleviating those of others, came soon to my rescue. Under my stern glance, Toddie gradually lost interest in his doll and its cradle, and began to thrust forth and outward his piteous lower lip, and to weep copiously.

"Dee Lord not make me sho bad," he cried through his tears. I doubt his having had any very clear idea of what he was saying, or whom he was addressing; but had the publican of whose prayer Toddie made so fair a paraphrase worn such a face when he offered his famous petition, it could not have been denied for a moment. Toddie even retired to a corner, and hid his face in self-imposed penance.

"Never mind, Toddie," said I sadly; "you didn't mean to do it, I know."

"I wantsh to love you," sobbed Toddie.

"Well, come here, you poor little fellow," said I, opening my arms, and wondering whether 'twas not after contemplation of some such sinner that good Bishop Tegner wrote:—

"Depths of love are atonement's depths, for love is atonement."

Toddie came to my arms, shed tears freely upon my shirt-front, and finally, after heaving a very long sigh, remarked:—

"Wantsh you to love me."

I complied with his request. Theoretically I had long believed that the higher wisdom of the Creator was most frequently expressed through the medium of his most innocent creations. Surely here was a confirmation of my theory, for who else had ever practically taught me the duty of the injured one toward his offender? I kissed Toddie and petted him, and at length succeeded in quieting him; his little face, in spite of much dirt and many tear-stains, was upturned with more of beauty in it than it ever held when its owner was full of joy; he looked earnestly, confidingly, into my eyes, and I congratulated myself upon the perfection of my forgiving spirit, when Toddie suddenly re-exhibited to me my old unregenerate nature, and the incompleteness of my forgiveness, by saying:—

"Kish my dolly, too."

"KISH MY DOLLY, TOO"

I obeyed. My forgiveness was made complete, but so was my humiliation. I abruptly closed our interview. We exchanged "God bless you's," according to Budge's instructions of the previous night, and at least one of the participants in this devotional exercise hoped the petitions made by the other were distinctly heard. Then I dropped into an easy-chair in the library, and fell to thinking. I found myself really and seriously troubled by the results of Toddie's operation with my bouquet. I might explain the matter to Miss Mayton—I undoubtedly could, for she was too sensible a woman to be easily offended merely by a ridiculous mistake, caused by a child. But she would laugh at me—how could she help it?—and to be laughed at by Miss Mayton was a something, the mere thought of which tormented me in a manner that made me fairly ashamed of myself. Like every other young man among young men, I had been the butt of many a rough joke, and had borne them without wincing; it seemed cowardly and contemptible that I should be so sensitive under the mere thought of laughter which would probably be heard by no one but Miss Mayton herself. But the laughter of a mere acquaintance is likely to lessen respect for the person laughed at. Heavens! the thought was unendurable! At any rate, I must write an early apology. When I was correspondent for the house with which I am now salesman, I reclaimed many an old customer who had wandered off—certainly I might hope, by a well-written letter, to regain in Miss Mayton's respect whatever position I had lost. I hastily drafted a letter, corrected it carefully, copied it in due form, and forwarded it by the faithful Michael. Then I tried to read, but without the least success. For hours I paced the piazza and consumed cigars; when at last I retired it was with many ideas, hopes, fears, and fancies which had never before been mine. True to my trust, I looked into my nephews' room; there lay the boys, in postures more graceful than any which brush or chisel have ever reproduced. Toddie, in particular, wore so lovely an expression that I could not refrain from kissing him. But I was none the less careful to make use of my new key, and to lock my other door also.

The next day was the Sabbath. Believing fully in the binding force and worldly wisdom of the Fourth Commandment, so far as it refers to rest, I have conscientiously trained myself to sleep two hours later on the morning of the holy day than I ever allowed myself to do on business days. But having inherited, besides a New England conscience, a New England abhorrence of waste, I regularly sit up two hours later on Saturday nights than on any others; and the night preceding this particular Sabbath was no exception to the rule, as the reader may imagine from the foregoing recital. At about 5.30 A.M., however, I became conscious that my nephews were not in accord with me on the Sinaitic law. They were not only awake, but were disputing vigorously, and, seemingly very loudly, for I heard their words quite distinctly. With sleepy condescension I endeavored to ignore these noisy irreverents, but I was suddenly moved to a belief in the doctrine of vicarious atonement, for a flying body, with more momentum than weight, struck me upon the not prominent bridge of my nose, and speedily and with unnecessary force accommodated itself to the outline of my eyes. After a moment spent in anguish, and in wondering how the missive came through closed doors and windows, I discovered that my pain had been caused by one of the dolls, which from its extreme uncleanness, I suspected belonged to Toddie; I also discovered that the door between the rooms was open.

"Who threw that doll?" I shouted, sternly.

There came no response.

"Do you hear?" I roared.

"What is it, Uncle Harry?" asked Budge, with most exquisitely polite inflection.

"Who threw that doll?"

"Huh?"

"I say, who threw that doll?"

"Why, nobody did it."

"Toddie, who threw that doll?"

"Budge did," replied Toddie, in muffled tones, suggestive of a brotherly hand laid forcibly over a pair of small lips.

"Budge, what did you do it for?"

"Why—why—I—because—why, you see—because, why, Toddie froo his dolly in my mouth; some of her hair went in, anyhow, an' I didn't want his dolly in my mouth, so I sent it back to him, an' the foot of the bed didn't stick up enough, so it went froo the door to your bed—that's what for."

The explanation seemed to bear marks of genuineness, albeit the pain in my eye was not alleviated thereby, while the exertion expended in eliciting the information had so thoroughly awakened me that further sleep was out of the question. Besides, the open door—had a burglar been in the room? No, my watch and pocket-book were undisturbed.

"Budge, who opened that door?"

After some hesitation, as if wondering who really did it, Budge replied:—

"Me."

"How did you do it?"

"Why, you see we wanted a drink, an' the door was fast, so we got out the window on the parazzo roof, an' comed in your window." (Here a slight pause.) "An' 'twas fun. An' then we unlocked the door, an' comed back."

Then I should be compelled to lock my window blinds—or theirs, and this in the summer season, too! Oh, if Helen could have but passed the house as that white-robed procession had filed along the piazza roof! I lay pondering over the vast amount of unused ingenuity that was locked up in millions of children, or employed only to work misery among unsuspecting adults, when I heard light footfalls at my bedside, and saw a small shape with a grave face approach and remark:

"I wants to come in your bed."

"What for, Toddie?"

"To fwolic; papa always fwolics us Sunday mornin's. Tum, Budgie, Ocken Hawwy's doin' to fwolic us."

TWO LITTLE SAVAGES
Budge replied by shrieking with delight, tumbling out of bed, and hurrying to that side of my bed not already occupied by Toddie. Then those two little savages sounded the onslaught and advanced precipitately upon me. Sometimes, during the course of my life, I have had day-dreams which I have told to no one. Among these has been one—not now so distinct as it was before my four years of campaigning—of one day meeting in deadly combat the painted Indian of the plains; of listening undismayed to his frightful war-whoop, and of exemplifying in my own person the inevitable result of the paleface's superior intelligence. But upon this particular Sunday morning I relinquished this idea informally but forever. Before the advance of these diminutive warriors I quailed contemptibly, and their battle-cry sent more terror to my soul than that member ever experienced from the well-remembered rebel yell. According to Toddie, I was going to "fwolic" them; but from the first they took the whole business into their own little but effective hands. Toddie pronounced my knees, collectively, "a horsie-bonnie." and bestrode them, laughing gleefully at my efforts to unseat him, and holding himself in position by digging his pudgy fingers into whatever portions of my anatomy he could most easily seize. Budge shouted," I want a horsie, too!" and seated himself upon my chest. "This is the way the horsie goes," explained he, as he slowly rocked himself backward and forward. I began to realize how my brother-in-law, who had once been a

31

fine gymnast, had become so flat-chested. Just then Budge's face assumed a more spirited expression, his eyes opened wide and lighted up, and shouting," This the way the horsie trots," he stood upright, threw up his feet, and dropped his forty-three avoirdupois pounds forcibly upon my lungs. He repeated this operation several times before I fully recovered from the shock conveyed by his combined impudence and weight; but pain finally brought my senses back, and with a wild plunge I unseated my demoniac riders and gained a clear space in the middle of the floor.

"Ah—h—h—h—h—h!" screamed Toddie; "I wants to ride horshie backen."

"Boo—oo—oo—oo—!" roared Budge; "I think you're real mean. I don't love you at all."

Regardless alike of Toddie's desires, of Budge's opinion and the cessation of his regard, I performed a hasty toilet. Notwithstanding my lost rest, I savagely thanked the Lord for Sunday; at church, at least, I could be free from my tormentors. At the breakfast table both boys invited themselves to accompany me to the sanctuary, but I declined, without thanks. To take them might be to assist somewhat in teaching them one of the best habits, but I strongly doubted whether the severest Providence would consider it my duty to endure the probable consequences of such an attempt. Besides I might meet Miss Mayton. I both hoped and feared I might, and I could not endure the thought of appearing before her with the causes of my pleasant remembrance. Budge protested, and Toddie wept, but I remained firm, although I was so willing to gratify their reasonable desires that I took them out for a long ante-service walk. While enjoying this little trip I delighted the children by killing a snake and spoiling a slender cane at the same time, my own sole consolation coming from the discovery that the remains of the staff were sufficient to make a cane for Budge. While returning to the house and preparing for church I entered into a solemn agreement with Budge, who was usually recognized as the head of this fraternal partnership. Budge contracted, for himself and brother, to make no attempts to enter my room; to refrain from fighting; to raise loose dirt only with a shovel, and to convey it to its destination by means other than their own hats and aprons; to pick no flowers; to open no water-faucets; to refer all disagreements to the cook, as arbitrator, and to build no houses of the new books which I had stacked upon the library table. In consideration of the promised faithful observance of these conditions, I agreed that Budge should be allowed to come alone to Sabbath-school, which convened directly after morning service, he to start only after Maggie had pronounced him duly cleansed and clothed. As Toddie was daily kept in bed from eleven till one, I felt that I might safely worship without distracting fears, for Budge could not alone, and in a single hour, become guilty of any particular sin. The church at Hillcrest had many more seats than members, and as but few summer visitors had yet appeared in the town, I was conscious of being industriously stared at by the native members of the congregation. This was of itself discomfort enough, but not all to which I was destined, for the usher conducted me quite near to the altar, and showed me into a pew whose only other occupant was Miss Mayton! Of course the lady did not recognize me—she was too carefully bred to do anything of the sort in church, and I spent ten uncomfortable minutes in mentally abusing the customs of good society. The beginning of the service partially ended my uneasiness, for I had no hymn-book—the pew contained none—so Miss Mayton kindly offered me a share in her own. And yet so faultlessly perfect and stranger-like was her manner that I wondered whether her action might not have been prompted merely by a sense of Christian duty; had I been the Khan of Tartary she could not have been more polite and frigid. The music to the first hymn was an air I had never heard before, so I stumbled miserably through the tenor, although Miss Mayton rendered the soprano without a single false note. The sermon was longer than I was in the habit of listening to, and I was frequently conscious of not listening at all. As for my position and appearance, neither ever seemed so insignificant as they did throughout the entire service.

MY NEPHEW BUDGE IN HIS BEST

The minister reached "And finally, dear brethren," with my earnest prayers for a successful and speedy finale. It seemed to me that the congregation sympathized with me, for there was a general rustle behind me as these words were spoken. It soon became evident, however, that the hearers were moved by some other feeling, for I heard a profound titter or two behind me. Even Miss Mayton turned her head with more alacrity than was consistent with that grace which usually characterized her motions, and the minister himself made a pause of unusual length, I turned in my seat, and saw my nephew Budge, dressed in his best, his head irreverently covered, and his new cane swinging in the most stylish manner. He paused at each pew, carefully surveyed its occupants, seemed to fail in finding the object of his search, but continued his efforts in spite of my endeavors to catch his eye. Finally he recognized a family acquaintance, and to him he unburdened his bosom by remarking, in tones easily heard throughout the church:—

"I want to find my uncle."

Just then he caught my eye, smiled rapturously, hurried to me, and laid his rascally soft cheek confidingly against mine, while an audible sensation pervaded the church. What to do or say to him I scarcely knew; but my quandary was turned to wonder, as Miss Mayton, her face full of ill-repressed mirth, but her eyes full of tenderness, drew the little scamp close to her, and kissed him soundly. At the same instant, the minister, not without some little hesitation, said, "Let us pray." I hastily bowed my head, glad of a chance to hide my face; but as I stole a glance at the cause of this irreligious disturbance, I caught Miss Mayton's eye. She was laughing so violently that the contagion was unavoidable, and I laughed all the harder as I felt that one mischievous boy had undone the mischief caused by another.

After the benediction, Budge was the recipient of a great deal of attention, during the confusion of which I embraced the opportunity to say to Miss Mayton:—

"Do you still sustain my sister in her opinion of my nephews, Miss Mayton?"

"I think they're too funny for anything," replied the lady, with great enthusiasm. "I do wish you would bring them to call upon me. I'm longing to see an original young gentleman."

"Thank you," said I. "And I'll have Toddie bring a bouquet by way of atonement."

"Do," she replied, as I allowed her to pass from the pew. The word was an insignificant one, but it made me happy once more.

33

"You see, Uncle Harry," exclaimed Budge, as we left the church together, "the Sunday-school wasn't open yet, an' I wanted to hear if they'd sing again in church; so I came in, an' you wasn't in papa's seat, an' I knew you was somewhere, so I looked for you."

"Bless you," thought I, snatching him into my arms as if to hurry him into Sabbath-school, but really to give him a kiss of grateful affection, "you did right—exactly right."

My Sunday dinner was unexceptional in point of quantity and quality, and a bottle of my brother-in-law's claret proved to be the most excellent; yet a certain uneasiness of mind prevented my enjoying the meal as thoroughly as under other circumstances I might have done. My uneasiness came of a mingled sense of responsibility and ignorance. I felt that it was the proper thing for me to see that my nephews spent the day with some sense of the requirements and duties of the Sabbath; but how I was to bring it about I hardly knew. The boys were too small to have Bible-lessons administered to them, and they were too lively to be kept quiet by any ordinary means. After a great deal of thought, I determined to consult the children themselves, and try to learn what their parents' custom had been.

"Budge," said I, "what do you do Sundays when your papa and mamma are home? What do they read to you—what do they talk about?"

"Oh, they swing us—lots!" said Budge, with brightening eyes.

"An' zey takes us to get jacks," observed Toddie.

"Oh, yes!" exclaimed Budge; "jacks-in-the-pulpit,—don't you know?"

"Hum—ye—es; I do remember some such thing in my youthful days; they grow where there's plenty of mud, don't they?"

"Yes, an' there's a brook there, an' ferns, an' birchbark, an' if you don't look out you'll tumble into the brook when you go to get birch."

"An' we goes to Hawksnest Rock," piped Toddie, "an' papa carries us up on his back when we gets tired."

"An' he makes us whistles," said Budge.

"Budge," said I, rather hastily, "enough. In the language of the poet

'These earthly pleasures I resign'

and I'm rather astonished that your papa hasn't taught you to do likewise. Don't he ever read to you?"

"Oh, yes," cried Budge, clapping his hands as a happy thought struck him. "He gets down the Bible—the great big Bible, you know—an' we all lay on the floor, an' he reads us stories out of it. There's David, an' Noah, an' when Christ was a little boy, an' Joseph, an' turn back Pharo's army hallelujah———"

"And what?"

"TurnbackPharo'sarmyhallelujah," repeated Budge. "Don't you know how Moses held his cane out over the Red Sea, an' the water went 'way up one side, an' 'way up the other side, and all the Isrulites went across? It's just the same thing as drown old Pharo's army hallelujah—don't you know."

"Budge," said I; "I suspect you of having, heard the Jubilee Singers."

"Oh, an' papa an' mamma sings us all those jubilee songs—there's 'Swing Low,' an' 'Roll Jordan,' an' 'Steal Away,' an' 'My Way's Cloudy,' an' 'Get on Board, Childuns,' an' lots. An' you can sing us every one of 'em."

"An' papa takes us in the woods and makesh us canes," said Toddie.

PUTTING AN EXTENSION ON THE AFTERNOON

"Yes," said Budge, "and where there's new houses buildin', he takes us up ladders."

"Has he any way of putting an extension on the afternoon?" I asked.

"I don't know what that is," said Budge, "but he puts an India-rubber blanket on the grass, and then we all lie down and make b'lieve we're soldiers asleep. Only sometimes when we wake up, papa stays asleep, an' mamma won't let us wake him. I don't think that's a very nice play."

"Well, I think Bible stories are nicer than anything else, don't you?"

Budge seemed somewhat in doubt. "I think swingin' is nicer," said he—"oh, no;— let's get some jacks—I'll tell you what!—make us whistles, an' we can blow on 'em while we're goin' to get the jacks. Toddie, dear, wouldn't you like jacks an' whistles?"

"Yesh—an' swingin'—an' birch—an' wantsh to go to Hawksnesh Rock," answered Toddie.

"Let's have Bible stories first," said I. "The Lord mightn't like it if you didn't learn anything good to-day."

"Well," said Budge, with the regulation religious-matter-of-duty face, "let's. I guess I like 'bout Joseph best."

"Tell us 'bout Bliaff," suggested Toddie.

"Oh, no, Tod," remonstrated Budge; "Joseph's coat was just as bloody as Goliath's head was." Then Budge turned to me and explained that "all Tod likes Goliath for is 'cause when his head was cut off it was all bloody." And then Toddie—the airy sprite

35

whom his mother described as being irresistibly drawn to whatever was beautiful—
Toddie glared upon me, as a butcher's apprentice might stare at a doomed lamb, and
remarked:—

"Bliaff's head was all bluggy, an' David's sword was all bluggy—bluggy as everyfing."

I hastily breathed a small prayer, opened the Bible, turned to the story of Joseph,
and audibly condensed it, as I read:

"Joseph was a good little boy, whose papa loved him very dearly. But his brothers
didn't like him. And they sold him to go to Egypt. And he was very smart, and told
people what their dreams meant, and he got to be a great man. And his brothers went to
Egypt to buy corn, and Joseph sold them some, and then he let them know who he was.
And he sent them home to bring their papa to Egypt, and then they all lived there
together."

"That ain't it," remarked Toddie, with the air of a man who felt himself to be
unjustly treated. "Is it, Budge?"

"Oh, no," said Budge, "you didn't read it good a bit; I'll tell you how it is. Once
there was a little boy named Joseph, an' he had eleven budders—they was awful eleven
budders. An' his papa gave him a new coat, an' his budders hadn't nothin' but their old
jackets to wear. An' one day he was carrying 'em their dinner, an' they put him in a deep,
dark hole, but they didn't put his nice new coat in—they killed a kid, an' dipped the
coat—just think of doin' that to a nice new coat—they dipped it in the kid's blood, an'
made it all bloody."

"All bluggy," echoed Toddie, with ferocious emphasis. Budge continued:—

"But there were some Ishmalites comin' along that way, and the awful eleven
budders took him out of the deep, dark hole, an' sold him to the Ishmalites, an' they sold
him away down in Egypt. An' his poor old papa cried, an' cried, an' cried, 'cause he
thought a big lion ate Joseph up; but he wasn't ate up a bit; but there wasn't no post-office
nor choo-choos,[6] nor stages in Egypt, an' there wasn't any telegraphs, so Joseph
couldn't let his papa know where he was; an' he got so smart an' so good that the king of
Egypt let him sell all the corn an' take care of the money; 'an one day some men came to
buy some com, an' Joseph looked at 'em 'an they was his own budders! An' he scared 'em
like everything; I'd have slapped 'em all if I'd been Joseph, but he just scared 'em, an' then
he let 'em know who he was, an' he kissed 'em an' he didn't whip 'em, or make 'em go
without their breakfast, or stand in a corner, nor none of them things; an' then he sent
them back for their papa, an' when he saw his papa comin', he ran like everything, and
gave him a great big hug and a kiss. Joseph was too big to ask him if he'd brought him any
candy, but he was awful glad to see him. An' the king gave Joseph's papa a nice farm, an'
they all had real good times after that."

[6] Railway cars.

"An' they dipped the coat in the blood, an' made it all bluggy," reiterated Toddie.

36

"Uncle Harry," said Budge, "what do you think my papa would do, if he thought I was all ate up by a lion? I guess he'd cry awful, don't you? Now tell us another story—oh, I'll tell you—read us 'bout—"

"'Bout Bliaff," interrupted Toddie.

"You tell me about him, Toddie," said I.

"Why," said Toddie, "Bliaff was a brate bid man, an' Dave was brate little man, an' Bliaff said, 'Come over here, an' I'll eat you up,' an' Dave said, 'I ain't fyaid of you.' So Dave put five little stones in a sling an' asked de Lord to help him, an' let ze sling go bang into bequeen Bliaff's eyes an' knocked him down dead, an' Dave took Bliaff's sword an' sworded Bliaff's head off, an' made it all bluggy, an' Bliaff runned away." This short narration was accompanied by more spirited and unexpected gestures than Mr. Gough ever puts into a long lecture.

"I don't like 'bout Goliath at all," remarked Budge, "I'd like to hear 'bout Ferus."

"Who?"

"Ferus; don't you know?"

"Never heard of him, Budge."

"IF I WAS ALL ATE UP BY A LION"
"Why—y—y—!" exclaimed Budge; "didn't you have no papa when you was a little boy?"

"Yes, but he never told me about any one named Ferus; there is no such person named in Anthon's Classical Dictionary, either. What sort of a man was he?"

"Why, once there was a man, an' his name was Ferus—Offerus, an' he went about fightin' for kings, but when any king got afraid of anybody, he wouldn't fight for him no more. An' one day he couldn't find no kings that wasn't afraid of nobody. An' the people told him the Lord was the biggest king in the world, an' he wasn't afraid of nobody nor nothing. An' he asked 'em where he could find the Lord, an' they said he was 'way up in heaven so nobody couldn't see him but the angels, but he liked folks to work for him instead of fight. So Ferus wanted to know what kind of work he could do, an' the people said there was a river not far off, where there wasn't no ferry-boats, 'cos the water run so fast, an' they guessed if he'd carry folks across, the Lord would like it. So Ferus went there, an' he cut him a good, strong cane, an' whenever anybody wanted to go across the river he'd carry 'em on his back.

"One night he was sittin' in his little house by the fire, and smokin' his pipe an' readin' the paper, an' 'twas rainin' an' blowin' an' hailin' an' stormin', an' he was so glad there wasn't anybody wantin' to go 'cross the river, when he heard somebody call out,

37

'Ferus!' An' he looked out the window, but he couldn't see nobody, so he sat down again. Then somebody called, 'Ferus!' again, and he opened the door again, an' there was a little bit of a boy, 'bout as big as Toddie. An' Ferus said, 'Hello, young fellow, does your mother know you're out?' An' the little boy said, 'I want to go 'cross the river.'—'Well,' says Ferus, 'you're a mighty little fellow to be travelin' alone, but hop up.' So the little boy jumped up on Ferus' back, and Ferus walked into the water. Oh, my—wasn't it cold? An' every step he took, the little boy got heavier, so Ferus nearly tumbled down an' they liked to both got drownded. An' when they got across the river Ferus said, 'Well, you are the heaviest small fry I ever carried,' an' he turned around to look at him, an' 'twasn't no little boy at all—'twas a big man—'twas Christ. An' Christ said, 'Ferus, I heard you was tryin' to work for me, so I thought I'd come down an' see you, an' not let you know who I was. An' now you shall have a new name; you shall be called Christofferus, 'cos that means Christ-carrier.' An' everybody called him Christofferus after that, an' when he died they called him Saint Christopher, 'cos Saint is what they call good people when they're dead."

Budge, himself, had the face of a rapt saint as he told this story, but my contemplation of his countenance was suddenly arrested by Toddie, who, disapproving of the unexciting nature of his brother's recital, had strayed into the garden, investigated a hornet's nest, been stung, and set up a piercing shriek. He ran in to me, and as I hastily picked him up, he sobbed:—

"Want to be wocked.[7] Want 'Toddie one boy day.'"

[7] Rocked

I rocked him violently, and petted him tenderly, but again he sobbed:—

"Want 'Toddie one boy day.'"

"What does the child mean?" I exclaimed.

"He wants you to sing to him about 'Charlie boy one day,'" said Budge. "He always wants mamma to sing that when he's hurt, an' then he stops crying."

"I don't know it," said I. "Won't 'Roll, Jordan,' do, Toddie?"

"I'll tell you how it goes," said Budge, and forthwith the youth sang the following song, a line at a time, I following him in words and air:—

"Where is my little bastik[8] gone?
Said Charley boy one day;
I guess some little boy or girl
Has taken it away.
"An' kittie, too—where ish she gone?
Oh, dear, what I shall do?
I wish I could my bastik find,
An' little kittie, too.
"I'll go to mamma's room an' look;

38

Perhaps she may be there;
For kittie likes to take a nap
In mamma's easy chair.
"O mamma, mamma, come an' look!
See what a little heap!
Here's kittie in the bastik here,
All cuddled down to sleep."
[8] Basket.

Where the applicability of this poem to my nephew's peculiar trouble appeared, I could not see, but as I finished it, his sobs gave place to a sigh of relief.

"Toddie," said I, "do you love your Uncle Harry?"

"Esh, I do love you."

"Then tell me how that ridiculous song comforts you?"

"Makes me feel good, an' all nicey," replied Toddie.

"Wouldn't you feel just as good if I sang, 'Plunged in a gulf of dark despair'?"

"No, don't like dokdishpairs; if a dokdishpair done anyfing to me, I'd knock it right down dead."

With this extremely lucid remark, our conversation on this particular subject ended; but I wondered, during a few uneasy moments, whether the temporary mental aberration which had once afflicted Helen's grandfather and mine was not reappearing in this, his youngest descendant. My wondering was cut short by Budge, who remarked, in a confidential tone:—

TODDIE INVESTIGATING A HORNET'S NEST
"Now, Uncle Harry, we'll have the whistles, I guess."

I acted upon the suggestion, and led the way to the woods. I had not had occasion to seek a hickory sapling before for years; not since the war, in fact, when I learned how hot a fire small hickory sticks would make. I had not sought wood for whistles since—— Gracious, nearly a quarter of a century ago! The dissimilar associations called up by these recollections threatened to put me in a frame of mind which might have resulted in a bad poem, had not my nephews kept up a lively succession of questions, such as no one but children can ask. The whistles completed, I was marched, with music, to the place where the "jacks" grew. It was just such a place as boys instinctively delight in—low, damp, and boggy, with a brook hiding treacherously away, under overhanging ferns and grasses. The children knew by sight the plant which bore the "jacks," and every discovery was announced by a piercing shriek of delight. At first, I looked hurriedly toward the brook as each yell clove the air; but, as I became accustomed to it, my attention was diverted by some exquisite ferns. Suddenly, however, a succession of shrieks announced that something was wrong, and across a large fern I saw a small face in a great deal of agony. Budge was hurrying to the relief of his brother, and was soon as deeply imbedded as Toddie was, in the rich black mud at the bottom of the brook. I dashed to the rescue, stood astride the brook, and offered a hand to each boy, when a treacherous tuft of grass gave way, and, with a glorious splash, I went in myself. This accident turned Toddie's sorrow to laughter, but I can't say I made light of my misfortune on that account. To fall into clean water is not pleasant, even when one is trout-fishing; but to be clad in white pants, and suddenly drop knee-deep in the lap of mother Earth is quite a different thing. I hastily picked up the children, and threw them upon the bank, and then wrathfully strode out myself, and tried to shake myself as I have seen a Newfoundland dog do. The shake was not a success—it caused my trouser-leg to flap dismally about my ankles, and sent the streams of loathsome ooze trickling down into my shoes. My hat, of drab felt, had fallen off by the brookside, and been plentifully spattered as I got out. I looked at my youngest nephew with speechless indignation.

"Uncle Harry," said Budge, "'twas real good of the Lord to let you be with us, else Toddie might have been drownded."

"Yes," said I, "and I shouldn't have much――"

"Ocken Hawwy," cried Toddie, running impetuously toward me, pulling me down, and patting my cheek with his muddy, black hand, "I loves you for taking me out de water."

"I accept your apology," said I, "but let's hurry home." There was but one residence to pass, and that, thank fortune, was so densely screened by shrubbery that the inmates could not see the road. To be sure, we were on a favorite driving-road, but we could reach home in five minutes, and we might dodge into the woods if we heard a carriage coming. Ha! There came a carriage already, and we—was there ever a sorrier-looking group? There were ladies in the carriage, too—could it be—of course it was—did the evil spirit, which guided those children always, send an attendant for Miss Mayton before he began operations? There she was, anyway—cool, neat, dainty, trying to look collected, but severely flushed by the attempt. It was of no use to drop my eyes, for she had already recognized me; so I turned to her a face which I think must have been just the one— unless more defiant—that I carried into two or three cavalry charges.

"You seem to have been having a real good time together," said she, with a conventional smile, as the carriage passed. "Remember, you're all going to call on me to-morrow afternoon."

"BUT LET'S HURRY HOME"

Bless the girl! Her heart was as quick as her eyes—almost any other young lady would have devoted her entire energy to laughing on such an occasion, but she took her earliest opportunity to make me feel at ease. Such a royal-hearted woman deserves to—I caught myself just here, with my cheeks growing quite hot under the mud Toddie had put on them, and I led our retreat with a more stylish carriage than my appearance could possibly have warranted, and then I consigned my nephews to the maid with very much the air of an officer turning over a large number of prisoners he had captured. I hastily changed my soiled clothing for my best—not that I expected to see anyone, but because of a sudden increase in the degree of respect I felt toward myself. When the children were put to bed, and I had no one but my thoughts for companions, I spent a delightful hour or two in imagining as possible some changes of which I had never dared to think before.

On Monday morning I was in the garden at sunrise. Toddie was to carry his expiatory bouquet to Miss Mayton that day, and I proposed that no pains should be spared to make his atonement as handsome as possible. I canvassed carefully every border, bed, and detached flowering plant until I had as accurate an idea of their possibilities as if I had inventoried the flowers in pen and ink. This done, I consulted the servant as to the unsoiled clothing of my nephews? She laid out the entire wardrobe for my inspection, and after a rigid examination of everything, I selected the suits which the boys were to wear in the afternoon. Then I told the girl that the boys were going with me after dinner to call on some ladies and that I desired that she should wash and dress them carefully.

"Tell me just what time you'll start, sir, and I'll begin an hour beforehand," said she. "That's the only way to be sure that they don't disgrace you."

For breakfast, we had, among other things, some stewed oysters served in soup-plates.

"O Tod," shrieked Budge, "there's the turtle-plates again—oh, ain't I glad!"

"Oo—ee—turtle pyates!" squealed Toddie.

"What on earth do you mean, boys?" I demanded.

"I'll show you," said Budge, jumping down from his chair, and bringing his plate of oysters cautiously toward me. "Now you just put your head down underneath my plate, and look up, and you'll see a turtle."

For a moment I forgot that I was not at a restaurant, and I took the plate, held it up, and examined its bottom.

"There!" said Budge, pointing to the trade-mark, in colors, of the makers of the crockery, "don't you see the turtle?"

I abruptly ordered Budge to his seat, unmoved even by Toddie's remark, that—

"Dey ish turtles, but dey can't kwawl awound like udder turtles."

After breakfast I devoted a great deal of fussy attention to myself. Never did my own wardrobe seem so meager and ill-assorted; never did I cut myself so many times while shaving; never did I use such unsatisfactory shoe-polish. I finally gave up in despair my effort to appear genteel, and devoted myself to the bouquet. I cut almost flowers enough to dress a church, and then remorselessly excluded every one which was in the least particular imperfect. In making the bouquet I enjoyed the benefit of my nephews' assistance and counsel, and took enforced part in conversation which flowers suggested.

"Ocken Hawwy," said Toddie, "ish heaven all like this, wif pretty f'owers? 'Cos I don't see what ze angels ever turns out for if 'tis."

"Uncle Harry," said Budge, "when the leaves all go up and down and wriggle around so, are they talking to the wind?"

"I—I guess so, old fellow."

"Who are you making that bouquet for, Uncle Harry?" asked Budge.

"For a lady—for Miss Mayton—that lady that saw us all muddy yesterday afternoon," said I.

"Oh, I like her," said Budge. "She looks so nice and pretty—just like a cake—just as if she was good to eat—oh, I just love her, don't you?"

"Well, I respect her very highly, Budge."

"'Spect? What does 'spect mean?"

"Why it means that I think she's a lady—a real pleasant lady—just the nicest sort of lady in the world—the sort of person I'd like to see every day, and like to see her better than anyone else."

"Oh, why, 'spect an' love means just the same thing, don't they, Uncle Har——"

"Budge," I exclaimed, somewhat hastily, "run, ask Maggie for a piece of string—quick!"

"All right," said Budge, moving off, "but they do, don't they?"

At two o'clock I instructed Maggie to dress my nephews, and at three we started to make our call. To carry Toddie's bouquet, and hold a hand of each boy so as to keep them from darting into the hedges for grasshoppers and the gutters for butterflies, was no easy work, but I managed to do it. As we approached Mrs. Clarkson's boarding-house I felt my hat was over one ear, and my cravat awry, but there was no opportunity to rearrange them, for I saw Alice Mayton on the piazza, and felt that she saw me. Handing the bouquet to Toddie, and promising him three sticks of candy if he would be careful and not drop it, we entered the garden. The moment we were inside the hedge and Toddie saw a man going over the lawn with a lawn-mower, he shrieked: "Oh, deresh a cutter-grass!" and dropped the bouquet with the carelessness born of perfect ecstasy. I snatched it before it reached the ground, dragged the offending youth up the walk, saluted Miss Mayton, and told Toddie to give the bouquet to the lady. This he succeeded in doing, but as Miss Mayton thanked him and stooped to kiss him he wriggled off the piazza like a little eel, shouted, "Turn on!" to his brother, and a moment later my nephews were following the "cutter-grass" at a respectful distance in the rear.

42

"Those are my sister's 'best children in the world,' Miss Mayton," said I.

"Bless the little darlings!" replied the lady; "I do love to see children enjoying themselves."

"So do I," said I, "when I'm not responsible for their well-being; but if the effort I've expended on those boys had been directed toward the interests of my employers, those worthy gentlemen would consider me invaluable."

Miss Mayton made some witty reply, and we settled to a pleasant chat about mutual acquaintances, about books, pictures, music and gossip of our set. I would cheerfully have discussed Herbert Spencer's system, the Assyrian Tablets, or any other dry subject with Miss Mayton, and felt that I was richly repaid by the pleasure of seeing her. Handsome, intelligent, composed, tastefully dressed, without a suspicion of the flirt or the languid woman of fashion about her, she awakened to the uttermost every admiring sentiment and every manly feeling. But, alas! my enjoyment was probably more than I deserved, so it was cut short. There were other ladies boarding at Mrs. Clarkson's, and, as Miss Mayton truthfully observed at our first meeting, men were very scarce at Hillcrest. So the ladies, by the merest accident, of course, happened upon the piazza and each one was presented to me, and common civility made it impossible for me to speak to Miss Mayton more than once in ten minutes. At any other time and place I should have found the meeting of so many ladies a delightful experience, but now——

Suddenly, a compound shriek arose from the lawn, and all the ladies sprang to their feet. I followed their example, setting my teeth firmly and viciously, hoping that whichever nephew had been hurt was badly hurt. We saw Toddie running toward us with one hand in his mouth, while Budge ran beside him, exclaiming:—

"Poor little Toddie! Don't cry! Does it hurt you awful? Never mind—Uncle Harry'll comfort you. Don't cry, Toddie, de-ar!"

Both boys reached the piazza steps, and clambered up, Budge exclaiming:—

"O Uncle Harry, Toddie put his fingers in the little wheels of the cutter-grass, an' it turned just the least little biddie, an' it hurted him."

But Toddie ran up to me, clasped my legs and sobbed: "Sing 'Toddie one boy day.'"

My blood seemed to freeze. I could have choked that dreadful child, suffering though he was. I stooped over him, caressed him, promised him candy, took out my watch and gave it to him to play with, but he returned to his original demand. A lady—the homeliest in the party—suggested that she should bind up his hand, and I inwardly blessed her, but he reiterated his request for "Toddie one boy day," and sobbed pitifully.

"What does he mean?" asked Miss Mayton.

43

"He wants Uncle Harry to sing, 'Charley boy one day,'" explained Budge; "he always wants that song when he's hurt anyway."

"Oh, do sing it to him, Mr. Burton," pleaded Miss Mayton; and all the other ladies exclaimed, "Oh, do!"

I wrathfully picked him up in my arms and hummed the air of the detested song.

"Sit in a wockin'-chair," sobbed Toddie.

I obeyed; and then my tormentor remarked:—

"You don't sing the wydes [words]—I wants the wydes."

I sang the words as softly as possible, with my lips close to his ear, but he roared:—

"Sing louder!"

"I don't know any more of it, Toddle," I exclaimed in desperation.

"Oh, I'll tell it all to you, Uncle Harry," said Budge. And there, before that audience, and her, I was obliged to sing that dreadful doggerel, line for line, as Budge repeated it. My teeth were set tight, my brow grew clammy, and I gazed upon Toddie with terrible thoughts in my mind. No one laughed—I grew so desperate that a titter would have given relief. At last I heard someone whisper:—

"See how he loves him! Poor man!—he's in perfect agony over the little fellow."

Had not the song reached its natural end just then, I believe I should have tossed my wounded nephew over the piazza rail. As it was, I set him upon his feet, announced the necessity of our departure, and began to take leave, when Miss Mayton's mother insisted that we should stay to dinner.

"For myself, I should be delighted, Mrs. Mayton," said I; "but my nephews have hardly learned company manners yet. I'm afraid my sister wouldn't forgive me if she heard I had taken them out to dinner."

"Oh, I'll take care of the little dears," said Miss Mayton; "they'll be good with me, I know."

"I couldn't be so unkind as to let you try it, Miss Mayton," I replied. But she insisted, and the pleasure of submitting to her will was so great that I would have risked even greater mischief. So Miss Mayton sat down to dinner with Budge upon one side and Toddie on the other, while I was fortunately placed opposite, from which position I could indulge in warning winks and frowns. The soup was served. I signaled the boys to tuck their napkins under their chins, and then turned to speak to the lady on my right. She politely inclined her head toward me, but her thoughts seemed elsewhere; following her eyes, I beheld my youngest nephew with his plate upraised in both hands, his head on the tablecloth, and his eyes turned painfully upward. I dared not speak, for fear he would drop the plate. Suddenly he withdrew his head, put on an angelic smile, tilted his plate so part of its contents sought refuge in the folds of Miss Mayton's dainty, snowy dress, while the offender screamed:—

"Oo-ee! zha turtle on my pyate!—Budgie, zha turtle on my pyate!"

"OO-EE! ZHA TURTLE ON MY PYATE"

Budge was about to raise his plate when he caught my eye and desisted. Poor Miss Mayton actually looked discomposed for the first time in her life, so far as I knew or could imagine. She recovered quickly, however, and treated that wretched boy with the most Christian forbearance and consideration during the remainder of the meal. When the dessert was finished she quickly excused herself, while I removed Toddie to a secluded corner of the piazza, and favored him with a lecture which caused him to howl pitifully, and compelled me to caress him and undo all the good which my rebukes had done. Then he and Budge removed themselves to the lawn, while I awaited Miss Mayton's reappearance to offer an apology for Toddie, and make our adieus. It was the custom of the ladies at Mrs. Clarkson's to stroll about the lovely rural walks after dinner and until twilight; and on this particular evening they departed in twos and threes, leaving me to make my apology without witnesses. I was rather sorry they went; it was not pleasant to feel that I was principally responsible for my nephew's blunder, and to have no opportunity to allay my conscience-pangs by conversation. It seemed to me Miss Mayton was forever in appearing; I even called up my nephews to have some one to talk to.

Suddenly she appeared, and in an instant I fervently blessed Toddie and the soup which the child had sent upon its aimless wanderings. I would rather pay the price of a fine dress than try to describe Miss Mayton's attire; I can only say that in style, color and ornament it became her perfectly, and set off the beauties of a face which I had never before thought was more than pleasing and intelligent. Perhaps the anger, which was excusable after Toddie's graceless caper, had something to do with putting unusual color into her cheeks, and a brighter sparkle than usual in her eyes. Whatever was the cause, she looked queenly, and I half imagined that I detected in her face a gleam of satisfaction at the involuntary start which her unexpected appearance caused me to make. She accepted my apology for Toddie with queenly graciousness, and then, instead of proposing that we should follow the other ladies, as a moment before I had hoped she would, she dropped into a chair. I accepted the invitation; the children should have been in bed half an hour before, but my sense of responsibility had departed when Miss Mayton appeared. The little scamps were safe until they should perform some new and unexpected act of impishness. They retired to one end of the piazza, and busied themselves in experiments upon a large Newfoundland dog, while I, the happiest man alive, talked to the glorious woman before me, and enjoyed the spectacle of her radiant beauty. The twilight came and deepened, but imagination prevented the vision from fading. With the coming of the darkness and the starlight, our voices unconsciously dropped to lower tones, and her voice seemed purest music. And yet we said nothing which all the world might not have listened to without suspecting a secret. The ladies returned in little groups, but either out of womanly intuition or in answer to my unspoken but fervent prayers, passed us and went into the house. I was affected by an odd mixture of desperate courage and despicable cowardice. I determined to tell her all, yet I shrank from the task with more terror than ever befell me in the first steps of a charge.

Suddenly a small shadow came from behind us and stood between us, and the voice of Budge remarked:—

"Uncle Harry 'spects you, Miss Mayton."

"Suspects me?—of what, pray?" exclaimed the lady, patting my nephew's cheek.

"Budge!" said I—I feel that my voice rose nearly to a scream—"Budge, I must beg of you to respect the sanctity of confidential communications."

"What is it, Budge?" persisted Miss Mayton. "You know the old adage, Mr. Burton: 'Children and fools speak the truth.' Of what does he suspect me, Budge?"

"'Taint sus-pect at all," said Budge, "it's es-pect."

"Expect?" echoed Miss Mayton.

"No, not 'ex,' it's es-pect. I know all about it, 'cause I asked him. Es-pect is what folks do when they think you're nice, and like to talk to you, and——"

"Respect is what the boy is trying to say, Miss Mayton," I interrupted, to prevent what I feared might follow. "Budge has a terrifying faculty for asking questions, and the result of some of them, this morning, was my endeavor to explain to him the nature of the respect in which gentlemen hold ladies."

"Yes," continued Budge, "I know all about it. Only Uncle Harry don't say it right. What he calls espect I calls love."

There was an awkward pause—it seemed an age. Another blunder, and all on account of those dreadful children. I could think of no possible way to turn the conversation; stranger yet, Miss Mayton could not do so, either. Something must be done—I could at least be honest, come what would—I would be honest.

"Miss Mayton," said I, hastily, earnestly, but in a very low tone. "Budge is a marplot, but he is a truthful interpreter for all that. But whatever my fate may be, please do not suspect me of falling suddenly in love for a holiday's diversion. My malady is of some months' standing. I——"

"I want to talk some" observed Budge. "You talk all the whole time. I—I—when I loves anybody, I kisses them."

Miss Mayton gave a little start, and my thoughts followed each other with unimagined rapidity. She did not turn the conversation—it could not be possible that she could not. She was not angry, or she would have expressed herself. Could it be that——

I bent over her, and acted upon Budge's suggestion. As she displayed no resentment, I pressed my lips a second time to her forehead, then she raised her head slightly, and I saw, in spite of darkness and shadows, that Alice Mayton had surrendered at discretion. Taking her hand and straightening myself to my full height, I offered to the Lord more fervent thanks than He ever heard from me in church. Then I heard Budge say, "I wants to kiss you, too," and I saw my glorious Alice snatch the little scamp into her arms, and treat him with more affection than I ever imagined was in her nature. Then she seized Toddie, and gave him a few tokens of forgiveness—I dare not think they were of gratitude.

Suddenly two or three ladies came upon the piazza.

"Come, boys," said I; "then I'll call with the carriage to-morrow at three, Miss Mayton. Good evening."

"Good evening," replied the sweetest voice in the world; "I'll be ready at three."

"Budge," said I, as soon as we were fairly outside the hedge-gate, "what do you like better than anything else in the world?"

"Candy," said Budge, very promptly.

"What next?"

"Oranges."

"What next?"

"Oh, figs, an' raisins, an' dear little kittie-kitties, an' drums, an' picture-books, an' little bakin' dishes to make mud-pies in, an' turtles, an' little wheelbarrows."

"Anything else?"

"Oh, yes—great big black dogs—an' a goat, an' a wagon for him to draw me in."

ACTING UPON BUDGES' SUGGESTION
Very well, old fellow—you shall have every one of those things to-morrow."

"Oh—h—h—h—h!" exclaimed Budge," I guess you're something like the Lord, ain't you?"

"What makes you think so, Budge?"

"Oh, 'cause you can do such lots of things at once. But ain't poor little Tod goin' to have noffin'?"

"Yes, everything he wants. What would you like, Toddie?"

"Wants a candy cigar," replied Toddie.

"What else?"

"Don't want nuffin' else—don't want to be boddered wif lots of fings."

The thoughts which were mine that night—the sense of how glorious a thing it is to be a man and be loved—the humility that comes with such a victory as I had gained—the rapid alternation of happy thoughts and noble resolutions—what man is there who does not know my whole story better than I can tell it? I put my nephews to bed; I told them every story they asked for; and when Budge, in saying his prayers, said, "an' bless that nice lady that Uncle Harry 'spects," I interrupted his devotions with a hearty hug. The children had been awake so far beyond their usual hour for retiring that they dropped asleep without giving any special notice of their intention to do so. Asleep, their faces were simply angelic. As I stood, candle in hand, gazing gratefully upon them, I remembered a sadly neglected duty. I hurried to the library and wrote the following to my sister:—

"Hillcrest. Monday Night.
"Dear Helen:—I should have written you before had I been exactly certain what to say about your boys. I confess that until now I have been blind to some of their virtues, and have imagined I detected an occasional fault. But the scales have fallen from my eyes, and I see clearly that my nephews are angels—positively angels. If I seem to speak extravagantly, I beg to refer you to Alice Mayton for collateral evidence. Don't come home at all—everything is just as it should be—even if you come, I guess I'll invite myself to spend the rest of the summer with you; I've changed my mind about its being a bore to live out of town and take trains back and forth every day. Ask Tom to think over such bits of real estate in your neighborhood as he imagines I might like.

"I repeat it, the boys are angels, and Alice Mayton is another, while the happiest man in the white goods trade is

"Your affectionate brother

"Harry."
Early next morning I sought the society of my nephews. It was absolutely necessary that I should overflow to some one—some one who was sympathetic and innocent and pure. I longed for my sister—my mother, but to some one I must talk at once. Budge fulfilled my requirements exactly; he was an excellent listener, very sympathetic by nature, and quick to respond. Not the wisdom of the most reverend sage alive could have been so grateful to my ear as that child's prattle was on that delightful morning. As for Toddie—blessed be the law of compensation!—his faculty of repetition, and of echoing whatever he heard said, caused him to murmur, "Miff Mayton, Miff Mayton," all morning long, and the sound gained in sweetness by its ceaseless iteration. To be sure, Budge took early and frequent occasions to remind me of my promises of the night before, and Toddie occasionally demanded the promised candy cigar; but these very interruptions only added joy to my own topic of interest each time it was resumed. The filling of

Budge's orders occupied two or three hours and all the vacant space in the carriage; even then the goat and goat-carriage were compelled to follow behind.

The program for the afternoon was arranged to the satisfaction of every one. I gave the coachman, Mike, a dollar to harness the goat and teach the children to drive him; this left me free to drive off without being followed by two small figures and two pitiful howls.

I always believed a horse was infected by the spirit of his driver. My dear old four-footed military companions always seemed to perfectly comprehend my desires and intentions, and certainly my brother-in-law's horses entered into my own spirits on this particular afternoon. They stepped proudly, they arched their powerful necks handsomely, their feet seemed barely to touch the ground; yet they did not grow restive under the bit, nor were they frightened, even, at a hideous steam road-rolling machine which passed us. As I drove up to Mrs. Clarkson's door I found that most of the boarders were on the piazza—the memories of ladies are usually good at times. Alice immediately appeared, composed of course, but more radiant than ever.

"Why, where are the boys?" she exclaimed.

"I was afraid they might annoy your mother," I replied, "so I left them behind."

"Oh, mother hardly feels well enough to go to-day," said she; "she is lying down."

"Then we can pick up the boys on the road," said I, for which remark my enchantress, already descending the steps, gave me a look which the ladies behind her would have given their best switches to have seen. We drove off as decorously as if it were Sunday and we were going to church; we industriously pointed out to each other every handsome garden and tasteful residence we passed; we met other people driving, and conversed fluently upon their horses, carriages and dress. But when we reached the edge of the town, and I turned into "Happy Valley," a road following the depressions and curves of a long, well-wooded valley, in which there was not a single straight line, I turned and looked into my darling's face. Her eyes met mine, and although they were full of a happiness which I had never seen in them before, they filled with tears, and their dear owner dropped her head on my shoulder.

TO SKIP ALL LOVE TALKS IN NOVELS

What we said on that long drive would not interest the reader. I have learned by experience to skip all love talks in novels, no matter how delightful the lovers may be. Recalling now our conversation, it does not seem to have had anything wonderful in it. I will only say, that if I had been happy on the evening before, my happiness now seemed to be sanctified; to be favored with the love and confidence of a simple girl scarcely past her childhood, is to receive a greater honor than court or field can bestow; but even this honor is far surpassed by that which comes to a man when a woman of rare intelligence, tact and knowledge of society and the world, unburdens her heart of all its hopes and fears, and unhesitatingly leaves her destiny to be shaped by his love. Women like Alice Mayton do not thus give themselves unreservedly away, except when their trust is born of knowledge as well as affection, and the realization of all this changed me on that afternoon from whatever I had been, into what I had long hoped I might one day be.

But the hours flew rapidly, and I reluctantly turned the horses' heads homeward. We had left almost the whole of "Happy Valley" behind us, and were approaching residences again.

"Now we must be very proper," said Alice.

"Certainly," I replied, "here's a good-by to happy nonsense for this afternoon."

I leaned toward her, and gently placed one arm about her neck; she raised her dear face, from which joy and trust had banished every indication of caution and reserve, my lips sought hers, when suddenly we heard a most unearthly, discordant shriek, which presently separated into two, each of which prolonged itself indefinitely. The horses started, and Alice—blessed be all frights now, henceforth and forevermore!—clung tightly to me. The sounds seemed to be approaching us, and were accompanied by a lively rattling noise, that seemed to be made by something wooden. Suddenly, as we approached a bend in the road, I saw my youngest nephew appear from some unknown space, describe a parabolic curve in the air, ricochet slightly from an earthy protuberance in the road, and make a final stop in the gutter. At the same time, there appeared from behind the bend, the goat, then the carriage dragging on one side, and, lastly, the boy Budge, grasping tightly the back of the carriage body, and howling frightfully. A direct collision between the carriage and a stone caused Budge to loose his hold, while the goat, after taking in the scene, trotted leisurely off, and disappeared in a road leading to the house of his late owner.

"Budge," I shouted, "stop that bawling and come here! Where's Mike?"

"He—boo—hoo—went to—boo—light—his—boo—hoo—hoo—pipe, an' I just let the—boo—hoo—whip go against to the goat, an' he scattooed."

"Nashty old goat scaddooed," said Toddie, in corroboration.

"Well, walk right home, and tell Maggie to wash and dress you," said I.

"O Harry," pleaded Alice, "after they've been in such danger! Come here to your own Aunt Alice, Budgie, dear,—and you, too, Toddie,—you know you said we could pick the boys up on the road, Harry. There, there—don't cry—let me wipe the ugly old dirt off you, and kiss the face, and make it well."

"Alice," I protested," don't let those dirty boys clamber all over you in that way."

"Silence, sir," said she, with mock dignity, "who gave me my lover, I should like to ask?"

So we drove up to the boarding-house with the air of people who had been devoting themselves to a couple of very disreputable children, and I drove swiftly away

50

again, lest the children should dispel the illusion. We soon met Mike, running. The moment he recognized us, he shouted:

"Ah, ye little dhivils,—beggin' yer pardon, Masther Harry, an' thankin' the Howly Mither that their good-for-nothin' little bones ain't broke to bits. Av they saw a hippypottymus hitched to Pharaoh's chariot they'd think 'emselves jist the byes to take the bossin' av it, the spalpeens!"

THE GOAT, THE CARRIAGE AND THE BOYS

But no number of ordinary hippopotami and chariots could have disturbed the heavenly tranquillity of my mind on this most glorious of evenings. Even a subtle sense of the fitness of things seemed to overshadow my nephews. Perhaps the touch of my enchantress did it; perhaps it came only from the natural relapse from great excitement; but no matter what the reason was, the fact remains that for the rest of the evening two very dirty suits of clothes held two children who gave one some idea of how the denizens of Paradise might seem and act. They even ate their suppers without indulging in any of the repulsive ways of which they had so large an assortment, and they did not surreptitiously remove from the table any fragments of bread and butter to leave on the piano, in the card-basket, and other places inappropriate to the reception of such varieties of abandoned property. They demanded a song after supper, but when I sang, "Drink to me only with Thine Eyes," and "Thou, Thou, Reign'st in this Bosom," they stood by with silent tongues and appreciative eyes. When they went to bed, I accompanied them by special invitation, but they showed no disposition to engage in the usual bedtime frolic and miniature pandemonium. Budge, when in bed, closed his eyes, folded his hands and prayed:—

"Dear Lord, bless papa an' mamma, an' Toddie, an' Uncle Harry, an' everybody else; yes, an' bless just lots that lovely, lovely lady that comforted me after the goat was bad to me, an' let her comfort me lots of times, for Christ's sake, Amen."

And Toddie wriggled, twisted, breathed heavily, threw his head back, and prayed:—

"Dee Lord, don't let dat old goat fro me into de gutter on my head aden, an' let Ocken Hawwy an' ze pitty lady be dere netst time I dets hurted."

Then the good-night salutations were exchanged, and I left the little darlings and enjoyed communion with my own thoughts, which were as peaceful and ecstatic as if the world contained no white goods houses, no doubtful customers, no business competition, no politics, gold rooms, stock-boards, doubtful banks, political scandals, personal iniquity nor anything which would prevent a short vacation from lasting through a long lifetime.

The next morning would have struck terror to the heart of any one but a newly accepted lover. Rain was falling fast, and in that steady, industrious manner which seemed to assert an intention to stick closely to business for the whole day. The sky was covered by one impenetrable, leaden cloud, water stood in pools in the streets which were soft with dust a few hours before; the flowers all hung their heads, like vagabonds who had been awake all night and were ashamed to face the daylight. Even the chickens stood about in dejected attitudes, and stray roosters from other poultry yards found refuge in

Tom's coop, without first being subjected to a trial of strength and skill by Tom's gamecock.

But no man in my condition of mind could be easily depressed by bad weather. I would rather have been able to drive about under a clear sky, or lounge under the trees, or walk to the post-office in the afternoon by the road which passed directly in front of Mrs. Clarkson's boarding-house; but man should not live for himself alone. In the room next mine, were slumbering two wee people to whom I owed a great deal, and who would mourn bitterly when they saw the condition of the skies and ground—I would devote myself to the task of making them so happy that they would forget the absence of sunshine out of doors—I would sit by their bedside and have a story ready for them the moment they awoke, and put them in such a good humor that they could laugh, with me, at cloud and rain.

I began at once to construct a story for their especial benefit; the scene was to be a country residence on a rainy day, and the actors two little boys who should become uproariously jolly in spite of the weather. Like most people not used to story-making, my progress was not very rapid; in fact, I had got no farther than the plot indicated above when an angry snarl came from the children's room.

"What's the matter, Budge?" I shouted, dressing myself as rapidly as possible.

"Ow—oo—ya—ng—um—boo—gaa!" was the somewhat complicated response.

"What did you say, Budge?"

"Didn't say noffin'."

"Oh—that's what I thought."

"Didn't thought."

"Budge,—Budge,—be good."

"Don't want to be good—ya—A—A!"

"Let's have some fun, Budge—don't you want to frolic?"

"No; I don't think frolics is nice."

"Don't you want some candy, Budge?"

"No—you ain't got no candy, I bleeve."

"Well, you sha'n't have any, if you don't stop being so cross."

The only reply to this was a mighty and audible rustling of the bedding in the boys' room, followed by a sound strongly resembling that caused by a slap; then came a prolonged wail, resembling that of an ungreased wagon wheel.

"What's the matter, Toddie?"

"Budge s'apped me—ah—h—h—h!"

"What made you slap your brother, Budge?"

"I didn't."

"You did!" screamed Toddie.

"I tell you I didn't—you're a naughty, bad boy to tell such lies, Toddie."

"What did you do, Budge?" I asked.

"Why—why—I was—I was turnin' over in bed, an' my hand was out, an' it tumbled against to Toddie—that's what."

By this time I was dressed and in the boys' room. Both my nephews were sitting up in bed, Budge looking as sullen as an old jailbird, and Toddie with tears streaming all over his face.

"Boys," said I, "don't be angry with each other—it isn't right. What do you suppose the Lord thinks, when He sees you so cross to each other?"

"He don't think noffin'," said Budge; "you don't think He can look through a black sky like that, do you?"

"He can look anywhere, Budge, and He feels very unhappy when He sees little brothers angry with each other."

"Well, I feel unhappy, too—I wish there wasn't never no old rain, nor noffin'."

"Then what would plants and flowers do for a drink and where would rivers come from for you to go sailing on?"

"An' wawtoo to mate mud-pies," added Toddie. "You's a naughty boy, Budgie"; and here Toddie's tears began to flow afresh.

"I ain't a bad boy, an' I don't want no old rain nohow, an' that's all about it. An' I don't want to get up, an' Maggie must bring me up my breakfast in bed."

"Boo—hoo—oo," wept Toddie, "wants my brepspup in bed too."

"Boys," said I, "now listen. You can't have any breakfast at all, unless you are up and dressed by the time the bell rings. The rising-bell rang some time ago. Now dress like

53

good boys, and you shall have some breakfast, and then you'll feel a great deal nicer, and then Uncle Harry will play with you and tell you stories all day long."

Budge crept reluctantly out of bed and caught up one of his stockings, while Toddie again began to cry.

"AN' WAWTOO TO MATE MUD-PIES"
"Toddie!" I shouted, "stop that dreadful racket, and dress yourself! What are you crying for?"

"Well, I feelsh bad."

"Well, dress yourself, and you'll feel better."

"Wantsh you to djesh me."

"Bring me your clothes, then—quick!"

Again the tears flowed copiously. "Don't want to bring 'em," said Toddie.

"Then come here!" I shouted, dragging him across the room and snatching up his tiny articles of apparel. I had dressed no small children since I was rather a small boy myself, and Toddies clothing confused me somewhat. I finally got something on him, when a contemptuous laugh from Budge interrupted me.

"How you goin' to put his shirt on under them things?" queried my oldest nephew.

"Budge," I retorted, "how are you going to get any breakfast if you don't put on something besides that stocking?"

The young man's countenance fell, and just then the breakfast-bell rang. Budge raised a blank face, hurried to the head of the stairs and shouted:—

"Maggie?"

"What is it, Budge?"

"Was—was that the rising-bell or the breakfast-bell?"

"'Twas the breakfast-bell."

There was dead silence for a moment, and then Budge shouted:—

"Well, we'll call that the risin'-bell. You can ring another bell for breakfast pretty soon, when I get dressed." Then this volunteer adjuster of household affairs came calmly back and commenced dressing in good earnest, while I labored along with Toddie's wardrobe.

"Where's the button-hook, Budge?" said I.

"It's—I—oh—um—I put it—say, Tod, what did you do with the button-hook yesterday?"

"Didn't hazh no button-hook," asserted Toddie.

"Yes, you did; don't you 'member how we was a playin' draw teef, an' the doctor's dog had the toofache, and I was pullin' his teef with the button-hook an' you was my little boy, an' I gived the toof-puller to you to hold for me? Where did you put it?"

"I'd no," replied Toddie, putting his hand in his pocket and bringing out a sickly-looking toad.

"Feel again," said I, throwing the toad out of the window, where it was followed by an agonized shriek from Toddie. Again he felt, and his search was rewarded by the tension-screw of Helen's sewing-machine. Then I attempted some research myself, and speedily found my fingers adhering to something of a sticky consistency. I quickly withdrew my hand, exclaiming:—

"What nasty stuff have you got in your pocket, Toddie?"

"'Tain't nashty 'tuff—it's byead an' lasses, an' it's nice, an' Budge an' me hazh little tea parties in de kicken-coop, an' we eats it, an' its dovely."

All this was lucid and disgusting, but utterly unproductive of button-hooks, and meanwhile the breakfast was growing cold. I succeeded in buttoning Toddie's shoes with my fingers, splitting most of my nails in the operation. I had been too busily engaged with Toddie to pay any attention to Budge, who I now found about half dressed and trying to catch flies on the window pane.

Snatching Toddie, I started for the dining-room, when Budge remarked reprovingly:

"Uncle Harry, you wasn't dressed when the bell rang, and you oughtn't to have any breakfast."

True enough—I was minus collar, cravat, and coat. Hurrying these on, and starting again, I was once more arrested:—

"Uncle Harry, must I brush my teeth this morning?"

"No—hurry up—come down without doing anything more, if you like, but come—it'll be dinner-time before we get breakfast."

55

Then that imp was moved, for the first time that morning to something like good-nature, and he exclaimed with a giggle:—

"My! What big stomachs we'd have when we got done, wouldn't we?"

At the breakfast table Toddie wept again, because I insisted on beginning operations before Budge came. Then neither boy knew exactly what he wanted. Then Budge managed to upset the contents of his plate into his lap, and while I was helping him to clear away the débris, Toddie improved the opportunity to pour his milk upon his fish and put several spoonfuls of oatmeal porridge into my coffee-cup. I made an early excuse to leave the table and turn the children over to Maggie. I felt as tired as if I had done a hard day's work, and was somewhat appalled at realizing that the day had barely begun. I lit a cigar and sat down to Helen's piano. I am not a musician, but even the chords of a hand-organ would have seemed sweet music to me on that morning. The music-book nearest to my hand was a church hymn-book, and the first air my eye struck was "Greenville." I lived once in a town, where, on a single day, a peddler disposed of thirty-eight accordions, each with an instruction-book in which this same air, under its original name, was the only air. For years after, a single bar of this air awakened the most melancholy reflections in my mind, but now I forgave all my musical tormentors as the familiar strains came comfortingly from the piano-keys. But suddenly I heard an accompaniment—a sort of reedy sound—and looking round, I saw Toddie again in tears. I stopped abruptly and asked:—

"What's the matter now, Toddie?"

"Don't want dat old tune; wantsh dancin' tune, so I can dance."

"WANTSH DANCIN' TUNE"
I promptly played "Yankee Doodle," and Toddie began to trot around the room with the expression of a man who intended to do his whole duty. Then Budge appeared, hugging a bound volume of "St. Nicholas." The moment that Toddie espied this he stopped dancing and devoted himself anew to the task of weeping.

"Toddie!" I shouted, springing from the piano stool, "what do you mean by crying at everything? I shall have to put you to bed again if you're going to be such a baby."

"That's the way he always does, rainy days," exclaimed Budge.

"Wantsh to see the whay-al what fwallowed Djonah," sobbed Toddie.

"Can't you demand something that's within the range of possibility, Toddie?" I mildly asked.

"The whale Toddie means is in this big red book; I'll find it for you," said Budge, turning over the leaves.

Suddenly a rejoicing squeal from Toddie announced that leviathan had been found, and I hastened to gaze. He was certainly a dreadful-looking animal, but he had an

56

enormous mouth, which Toddie caressed with his pudgy little hand, and kissed with tenderness, murmuring as he did so:—

"Dee old whay-al, I loves you. Is Djonah all goneded out of you 'tomach, whay-al? I finks 'twas weal mean in Djonah to get froed up when you hadn't noffin' else to eat, poor old whay-al."

"Of course Jonah's gone," said Budge, "he went to heaven long ago—pretty soon after he went to Nineveh an' done what the Lord told him to do. Now swing us, Uncle Harry."

The swing was on the piazza under cover from the rain; so I obeyed. Both boys fought for the right to swing first, and when I decided in favor of Budge, Toddie went off weeping, and declaring that he would look at his dear whay-al anyhow. A moment later his wail changed to a piercing shriek; and, running to his assistance, I saw him holding one finger tenderly and trampling on a wasp.

"What's the matter, Toddie?"

"Oo—oo—ee—ee—ee—ee—I putted my finger on a waps, and—oo—oo—the nasty old waps—oo—bited me. An' I don't like wapses a bit, but I likes whay-als—oo—ee—ee."

A happy thought struck me. "Why don't you boys make believe that big packing-box in your play-room is a whale?" said I.

A compound shriek of delight followed the suggestion, and both boys scrambled upstairs, leaving me a free man again. I looked remorsefully at the tableful of books which I had brought to read, and had not looked at for a week. Even now my remorse did not move me to open them—I found myself, instead, attracted toward Tom's library, and conning the titles of novels and volumes of poems. My eye was caught by "Initials," a love story which I had always avoided because I had heard impressionable young ladies rave about it; but now I picked it up and dropped into an easy chair. Suddenly I heard Mike, the coachman, shouting:—

"Go 'way from there, will ye? Ah, ye little spalpeen, it's good for ye that yer fahder don't see ye perched up dhere. Go 'way from dhat, or I'll be tellin' yer uncle."

"Don't care for nashty old uncle," piped Toddie's voice.

I laid down my book with a sigh, and went into the garden. Mike saw me and shouted:

"Mister Burthon, will you look dhere? Did ye's ever see the loike av dhat bye?"

Looking up at the play-room window, a long, narrow sort of loop-hole in a Gothic gable, I beheld my youngest nephew standing upright on the sill.

"Toddie, go in—quick!" I shouted, hurrying under the window to catch him in case he fell outward.

"I tan't!" squealed Toddie.

"Mike, run upstairs and snatch him in! Toddie, go in, I tell you!"

"Tell you I tan't doe in," repeated Toddie. "Ze bid bots ish ze whay-al, an' I'ze Djonah, an' ze whay-al's froed me up, an' I'ze dot to 'tay up here else ze whay-al 'ill fwallow me aden."

"I won't let him swallow you. Get in now—hurry," said I.

"Will you give him a penny not to fwallow me no more?" queried Toddie.

"Yes—a whole lot of pennies."

"Aw wight. Whay-al, don't you fwallow me no more, an' zen my Ocken Hawwy div you whole lots of pennies. You must be weal dood whay-al now, an' then I buys you some tandy wif your pennies, an'——"

Just then two great hands seized Toddie's frock in front, and he disappeared with a howl, while I, with the first feeling of faintness I had ever experienced, went in search of hammer, nails, and some strips of board, to nail on the outside of the window-frame. But boards could not be found, so I went up to the play-room and began to knock a piece or two off the box which had done duty as whale. A pitiful scream from Toddie caused me to stop.

"You're hurtin' my dee old whay-al; you's breakin' his 'tomach all open—you's a baddy man—'top hurtin' my whay-al, ee—ee—ee!" cried my nephew.

"I'm not hurting him, Toddie," said I. "I'm making his mouth bigger, so he can swallow you easier."

TWO GREAT HANDS SEIZED TODDIE
A bright thought came into Toddie's face and shone through his tears. "Then he can fwallow Budgie too, an' there'll be two Djonahs—ha—ha—ha! Make his mouf so big he can fwallow Mike, an' zen mate it 'ittle aden, so Mike tan't det out; nashty old Mike!"

I explained that Mike would not come upstairs again, so I was permitted to depart after securing the window.

Again I settled myself with book and cigar; there was at least for me the extra enjoyment that comes from the sense of pleasure earned by honest toil. Pretty soon Budge entered the room. I affected not to notice him, but he was not in the least abashed by my neglect.

58

"Uncle Harry," said he, throwing himself in my lap, between my book and me, "I don't feel a bit nice."

"What's the matter, old fellow?" I asked. Until he spoke I could have boxed his ears with great satisfaction to myself; but there is so much genuine feeling in whatever Budge says that he commands respect.

"Oh, I'm tired of playin' with Toddie, an' I feel lonesome. Won't you tell me a story?"

"Then what'll poor Toddie do, Budge?"

"Oh, he won't mind—he's got a dead mouse to be Jonah now, so I don't have no fun at all. Won't you tell me a story?"

"Which one?"

"Tell me one that I never heard before at all."

"Well, let's see; I guess I'll tell——"

"Ah—ah—ah—ah—ee—ee—ee!" sounded afar off, but fatefully. It came nearer—it came down the stairway and into the library, accompanied by Toddie, who, on spying me, dropped his inarticulate utterance, held up both hands, and exclaimed:—

"Djonah bwoke he tay-al!"

True enough; in one hand Toddie held the body of a mouse, and in the other that animal's caudal appendage; there was also perceptible, though not by the sense of sight, an objectionable odor in the room.

"HE'S GOT A DEAD MOUSE TO BE JONAH NOW"
"Toddie," said I, "go throw Jonah into the chicken coop, and I'll give you some candy."

"Me too," shouted Budge, "'cos I found the mouse for him."

I made both boys happy with candy, exacted a pledge not to go out in the rain, and then, turning them loose on the piazza, returned to my book. I had read, perhaps, half a dozen pages, when there arose and swelled rapidly in volume a scream from Toddie. Madly determined to put both boys into chairs, tie them, and clap adhesive plaster over their mouths, I rushed out upon the piazza.

"Budgie tried to eat my candy," complained Toddie.

"I didn't," said Budge.

"What did you do?" I demanded.

"I didn't bite it at all—I only wanted to see how it would feel between my teeth—that's all."

I felt the corners of my mouth breaking down, and hurried back to the library, where I spent a quiet quarter of an hour in pondering over the demoralizing influence exerted upon principle by a sense of the ludicrous. For some time afterward the boys got along without doing anything worse than make a dreadful noise, which caused me to resolve to find some method of deadening piazza floors if I ever owned a house in the country. In the occasional intervals of comparative quiet, I caught snatches of very funny conversation. The boys had coined a great many words whose meaning was evident enough, but I wondered greatly why Tom and Helen had never taught them the proper substitutes.

Among others was the word "deader," whose meaning I could not imagine. Budge shouted:—

"O Tod! there comes a deader! See where all them things like rooster's tails are a-shakin'?—Well, there's a deader under them."

"Datsh funny," remarked Toddie.

"An' see all the peoples a-comin' along," continued Budge, "they know 'bout the deader, an' they're goin' to see it fixed. Here it comes. Hello, deader!"

"Hay-oh, deader!" echoed Toddie.

What could "deader" mean?

"Oh, here it is right in front of us," cried Budge, "and ain't there lots of people? An' two horses to pull the deader—some deaders has only one."

My curiosity was too much for my weariness; I went to the front window, and, peering through, saw—a funeral procession! In a second I was on the piazza, with my hands on the children's collars; a second later two small boys were on the floor of the hall, the front door was closed, and two determined hands covered two threatening little mouths.

When the procession had fairly passed the house, I released the boys and heard two prolonged howls for my pains. Then I asked Budge if he wasn't ashamed to talk that way when a funeral was passing.

"'Twasn't a funeral," said he, "'Twas only a deader, an' deaders can't hear noffin'."

"But the people in the carriages could," said I.

"Well," said he, "they were so glad that the other part of the deader had gone to heaven that they didn't care what I said. Everbody's glad when the other part of deaders

60

go to heaven. Papa told me he was glad dear little Phillie was in heaven, an' I was, but I do want to see him again awful."

"Wantsh to shee Phillie aden awfoo," said Toddie, as I kissed Budge and hurried off to the library, unfit just then to administer further instruction or reproof. Of one thing I was very certain—I wished the rain would cease falling, so the children could go out of doors, and I could get a little rest, and freedom from responsibility. But the skies showed no sign of being emptied, the boys were snarling on the stairway, and I was losing my temper quite rapidly.

Suddenly I bethought me of one of the delights of my own childish days—the making of scrap-books. One of Tom's library drawers held a great many Lady's Journals. Of course Helen meant to have them bound, but I could easily re-purchase the numbers for her; they would cost two or three dollars, but peace was cheap at that price. On a high shelf in the play-room I had seen some supplementary volumes of "Mercantile Agency" reports, which would in time reach the rag-bag; there was a bottle of mucilage in the library desk, and the children owned an old pair of scissors. Within five minutes I had located two happy children on the bath-room floor, taught them to cut out pictures (which operation I quickly found they understood as well as I did) and to paste them into the extemporized scrap-book. Then I left them, recalling something from Newman Hall's address on the "Dignity of Labor." Why hadn't I thought before of showing my nephews some way of occupying their minds and hands? Who could blame the helpless little things for following every prompting of their unguided minds? Had I not a hundred times been told, when sent to the woodpile or the weediest part of the garden in my youthful days, that

"Satan finds some mischief still
For idle hands to do?"
Never again would I blame the children for being mischievous when their minds were neglected.

I spent a peaceful, pleasant hour over my novel, when I felt that a fresh cigar would be acceptable. Going upstairs in search of one, I found that Budge had filled the bath-tub with water, and was sailing boats, that is, hair-brushes.

Even this seemed too mild an offense to call for a rebuke, so I passed on without disturbing him, and went to my own room. I heard Toddie's voice, and having heard from my sister that Toddie's conversations with himself were worth listening to, I paused outside the door. I heard Toddie softly murmur:—

"Zere, pitty yady, 'tay zere. Now, 'ittle boy, I put you wif your mudder, 'tause mudders like zere 'ittle boys wif zem. An' you s'all have 'ittle sister tudder side of you,— zere. Now, 'ittle boy's an' 'ittle girl's mudder, don't you feel happy?—isn't I awfoo good to give you your 'ittle tsilderns? You ought to say, 'Fank you, Toddie,—you's a nice, fweet 'ittle djentleman.'"

I peered cautiously—then I entered the room hastily. I didn't say anything for a moment, for it was impossible to do justice impromptu, to the subject. Toddie had a progressive mind—if pictorial ornamentation was good for old books, why should not similar ornamentation be extended to objects more likely to be seen? Such may not have been Toddie's line of thought, but his recent operations warranted such a supposition. He had cut out a number of pictures, and pasted them upon the wall of my room—my sister's darling room, with its walls tinted exquisitely in pink. As a member of a hanging committee, Toddie would hardly have satisfied taller people, but he had arranged the pictures quite regularly, at about the height of his own eyes, had favored no one artist more than another, and had hung indiscriminately figure pieces, landscapes, and genre pictures. The temporary break of wall-line occasioned by the door communicating with his own room he had overcome by closing the door and carrying a line of pictures across its lower panels. Occasionally a picture fell off the wall, but the mucilage remained faithful, and glistened with its fervor of devotion. And yet so untouched was I by this artistic display, that when I found strength to shout, "Toddie," it was in a tone which caused this industrious amateur decorator to start violently, and drop his mucilage bottle, open end first, upon the carpet.

"What will mamma say?" I asked.

Toddie gazed, first blankly, and then inquiringly, into my face; finding no answer or sympathy there he burst into tears, and replied:—

"I dunno."

The ringing of the lunch bell changed Toddie from a tearful cherub into a very practical, business-like boy, and shouting, "Come on, Budge!" he hurried downstairs, while I tormented myself with wonder as to how I could best and most quickly undo the mischief Toddie had done.

I will concede to my nephews the credit of keeping reasonably quiet during meals; their tongues, doubtless, longed to be active in both the principal capacities of those useful members, but they had no doubt as to how to choose between silence and hunger. The result was a reasonably comfortable half-hour. Just as I began to cut a melon, Budge broke the silence by exclaiming:—

"O Uncle Harry, we haven't been out to see the goat to-day!"

"Budge," I replied, "I'll carry you out there under an umbrella after lunch, and you may play with that goat all the afternoon, if you like."

"Oh, won't that be nice?" exclaimed Budge. "The poor goat! he'll think I don't love him a bit, 'cause I haven't been to see him to-day. Does goats go to heaven when they die, Uncle Harry?"

"Guess not—they'd make trouble in the golden streets I'm afraid."

"Oh, dear! then Phillie can't see my goat. I'm so awful sorry," said Budge.

"I can see your goat, Budgie," suggested Toddie.

"Huh!" said Budge, very contemptuously. "You ain't dead."

"Well, Izhe goin' to be dead some day, an' zen your nashty old goat sha'n't see me a bit—see how he like zat." And Toddie made a ferocious attack on a slice of melon nearly as large as himself.

After lunch, Toddie was sent to his room to take his afternoon nap, and Budge went to the barn on my shoulders. I gave Mike a dollar, with instructions to keep Budge in sight, to keep him from teasing the goat, and to prevent his being impaled or butted. Then I stretched myself on a lounge and wondered whether only half a day of daylight had elapsed since I and the most adorable woman in the world had been so happy together. How much happier I would be when next I met her! The very torments of this rainy day would make my joy seem all the dearer and more intense. I dreamed happily for a few moments with my eyes open, and then somehow they closed, without my knowledge. What put into my mind the wreck scene from the play of "David Copperfield," I don't know; but there it came, and in my dream I was sitting in the balcony at Booth's, and taking a proper interest in the scene, when it occurred to me that the thunder had less of reverberation and more woodenness than good stage thunder should have. The mental exertion I underwent on this subject disturbed the course of my nap, but as wakefulness returned, the sound of the poorly simulated thunder did not cease; on the contrary, it was just as noisy, and more hopelessly a counterfeit than ever. What could the sound be? I stepped through the window to the piazza, and the sound was directly over my head. I sprang down the terrace and out upon the lawn, looked up, and beheld my youngest nephew strutting back and forth on the tin roof of the piazza, holding over his head a ragged old parasol. I roared:—"Go in, Toddie—this instant!"

The sound of my voice startled the young man so severely that he lost his footing, fell, and began to roll toward the edge and to scream, both operations being performed with great rapidity. I ran to catch him as he fell, but the outer edge of the water trough was high enough to arrest his progress, though it had no effect in reducing the volume of his howls.

"Toddie," I shouted, "lie perfectly still until uncle can get to you! Do you hear?"

HOLDING OVER HIS HEAD A RAGGED PARASOL
"Ess, but don't want to lie 'till," came in reply from the roof.

"'Tan't shee noffin' but sky an' wain."

"Lie still," I reiterated, "or I'll whip you dreadfully." Then I dashed upstairs, removed my shoes, climbed out and rescued Toddie, shook him soundly, and then shook myself.

"I wash only djust pyayin mamma, an' walkin' in ze wain wif an umbayalla," Toddie explained.

I threw him upon his bed and departed. It was plain that neither logic, threats, nor the presence of danger could keep this dreadful child from doing whatever he chose; what other means of restraint could be employed? Although not as religious a man as my good mother could wish, I really wondered whether prayer, as a last resort, might not be effective. For his good and my own peace, I would cheerfully have read through the whole prayer-book. I could hardly have done it just then, though, for Mike solicited an audience at the back door, and reported that Budge had given the carriage sponge to the goat, put handfuls of oats into the pump cylinder, pulled hairs out of the black mare's tail, and with a sharp nail drawn pictures on the enamel of the carriage-body. Budge made no denial, but looked very much aggrieved, and remarked that he couldn't never be happy without somebody having to go get bothered; and he wished there wasn't nobody in the world but organ-grinders and candy-store men. He followed me into the house, flung himself into a chair, put on a look which I imagine Byron wore before he was old enough to be malicious, and exclaimed:—

"I don't see what little boys was made for, anyhow; if ev'rybody gets cross with them, an' don't let 'em do what they want to. I'll bet when I get to heaven, the Lord won't be as ugly to me as Mike is,—an' some other folks, too. I wish I could die and be buried right away,—me an' the goat—an' go to heaven, where we wouldn't be scolded."

Poor little fellow! First I laughed inwardly at his idea of heaven, and then I wondered whether my own was very different from it, or any more creditable. I had no time to spend, however, even in pious reflection. Budge was quite wet, his shoes were soaking, and he already had an attack of catarrh; so I took him to his room and redressed him, wondering all the while how much similar duties my own father had had to do for me had shortened his life, and how with such a son as I was, he lived as long as he did. The idea that I was in some slight degree atoning for my early sins, so filled my thoughts that I did not at first notice the absence of Toddie. When it did become evident to me that my youngest nephew was not in the bed in which I had placed him, I went in search of him. He was in none of the chambers, but hearing gentle murmurs issue from a long, light closet, I looked in and saw Toddie sitting on the floor, and eating the cheese out of a mouse-trap. A squeak of my boots betrayed me, and Toddie, equal to the emergency, sprang to his feet and exclaimed:—

"I didn't hurt de 'ittle mousie one bittie; I just letted him out, and he runded away."

"I DIDN'T HURT DE 'ITTLE MOUSIE"
And still it rained. Oh, for a single hour of sunlight, so that the mud might be only damp dirt, and the children could play without tormenting other people! But it was not to be; slowly, and by the aid of songs, stories, an improvised menagerie, in which I personated every animal, besides playing ostrich and armadillo, and with a great many disagreements, the afternoon wore to its close, and my heart slowly lightened. Only an hour or two more, and the children would be in bed for the night, and then I would enjoy, in unutterable measure, the peaceful hours which would be mine. Even now they were inclined to behave themselves; they were tired and hungry, and stretched themselves on the floor to await dinner. I embraced the opportunity to return to my book, but I had hardly read a page, when a combined crash and scream summoned me to the dining-room. On the floor lay Toddie, a great many dishes, a roast leg of lamb, several ears of green corn, the butter-dish and its contents, and several other misplaced edibles. One thing was quite evident; the scalding contents of the gravy-dish had been emptied on Toddie's arm, and how severely the poor child might be scalded I did not know. I hastily

split open his sleeve from wrist to shoulder, and found the skin very red; so, remembering my mother's favorite treatment for scalds and burns, I quickly spread the contents of a dish of mashed potato on a clean handkerchief, and wound the whole around Toddie's arm as a poultice. Then I demanded an explanation.

"I was only djust reatchin' for a pieshe of bwed," sobbed Toddie, "an' then the bad old tabo beginded to froe all its fings at me, an' tumble down bang."

He undoubtedly told the truth as far as he knew it; but reaching over tables is a bad habit in small boys, especially when their mothers cling to old-fashioned heirlooms of tables, which have folding leaves; so I banished Toddie to his room, supperless, to think of what he had done. With Budge alone, I had a comfortable dinner off the salvage from the wreck caused by Toddie, and then I went upstairs to see if the offender had repented. It was hard to tell, by sight, whether he had or not, for his back was to me, as he flattened his nose against the window, but I could see that my poultice was gone.

"Where is what uncle put on your arm, Toddie?" I asked.

"I ate it up," said the truthful youth.

"Did you eat the handkerchief, too?"

"No; I froed nashty old handkerchief out the window—don't want dirty old handkerchiefs in my nice 'ittle room."

I was so glad that his burn had been slight that I forgave the insult to my handkerchief, and called up Budge, so that I might at once get both boys into bed, and emerge from the bondage in which I had lived all day long. But the task was no easy one. Of course my brother-in-law, Tom Lawrence, knows better than any other man the necessities of his own children, but no children of mine shall ever be taught so many methods of imposing upon parental good-nature. Their program called for stories, songs, moral conversations, frolics, the presentation of pennies, the dropping of the same, at long intervals, into tin savings-banks, followed by a deafening shaking-up of both banks; then a prayer must be offered, and no conventional one would be tolerated; then the boys performed their own devotions, after which I was allowed to depart with an interchange of "God bless yous." As this evening I left the room with their innocent benedictions sounding in my ears, a sense of personal weakness, induced by the events of the day, moved me to fervently respond "Amen!"

A TRIBUTE TO MOTHERS

Mothers of American boys, accept from me a tribute of respect, which no words can fitly express—of wonder greater than any of the great things of the world ever inspired—of adoration as earnest and devout as the Catholic pays to the Virgin. In a single day, I, a strong man, with nothing else to occupy my mind, am reduced to physical and mental worthlessness by the necessities of two boys not overmischievous or bad. And you—Heaven only knows how—have unbroken weeks, months, years, yes, lifetimes of just such experiences, and with them the burden of household cares, of physical ills and depressions, of mental anxieties that pierce thy hearts with as many sorrows as grieved the

65

Holy Mother of old. Compared with thy endurance, that of the young man, the athlete, is as weakness; the secret of thy nerves, wonderful even in their weakness, is as great as that of the power of the winds. To display decision, thy opportunities are more frequent than those of the greatest statesmen; thy heroism laughs into insignificance that of fort and field; thou art trained in a school of diplomacy such as the most experienced court cannot furnish. Do scoffers say thou canst not hold the reins of government? Easier is it to rule a band of savages than to be the successful autocrat of thy little kingdom. Compared with the ways of men, even thy failures are full of glory. Be thy faults what they may, thy one great, mysterious, unapproachable success places thee, in desert, far above warrior, ruler or priest.

The foregoing soliloquy passed through my mind as I lay upon the bed where I had thrown myself after leaving the children's room. Whatever else attempted to affect me mentally, found my mind a blank until the next morning, when I awoke to realize that I had dropped asleep just where I fell, and that I had spent nearly twelve hours lying across a bed in an uncomfortable position, and without removing my daily attire. My next impression was that quite a bulky letter had been pushed under my chamber-door. Could it be that my darling—I hastily seized the envelope and found it addressed in my sister's writing, and promising a more voluminous letter than that lady had ever before honored me with. I opened it, dropping an enclosure which, doubtless, was a list of necessities which I would please pack, etc. and read as follows:—

July 1, 1875.
"My Dear Old Brother:—Wouldn't I like to give you the warmest of sisterly hugs? I can't believe it, and yet I am in ecstasies over it. To think that you should have got that perfection of a girl, who has declined so many great catches—you, my sober, business-like, unromantic big brother—oh, it's too wonderful! But now I think of it, you are just the people for each other. I'd like to say that it's just what I'd always longed for, and I invited you to Hillcrest to bring it about; but the trouble with such a story would be that it wouldn't have a word of truth in it. You always did have a faculty for doing just what you pleased, and what nobody ever expected you to do, but now you've exceeded yourself.

"And to think that my little darlings played an important part in bringing it all about! I shall take the credit of that, for if it hadn't been for me who would have helped you, sir? I shall expect you to remember both of them handsomely at Christmas.

"I don't believe I am guilty of breach of confidence in sending the enclosed, which I have just received from my sister-in-law that is to be. It will tell you some causes of your success of which you, with a man's conceit, haven't imagined for a minute, and it will tell you, too, of a maiden's first and natural fear under such circumstances—a fear which I know you, with your honest, generous heart, will hasten to dispel. As you're a man, you're quite likely to be too stupid to read what's written between the lines; so I'd better tell you that Alice's fear is that in letting herself go so easily, she may have seemed to lack proper reserve and self-respect. You don't need to be told that no woman alive has more of these very qualities.

"Bless your dear old heart, Harry,—you deserve to be shaken to death if you're not the happiest man alive. I must hurry home and see you both with my own eyes, and learn to believe that all this wonderful, glorious thing has come to pass. Give Alice a sister's kiss for me (if you know how to give more than one kind), and give my cherubs a hundred each from the mother that wants to see them so much.

"With love and congratulations,

"Helen."

The other letter, which I opened with considerable reverence and more delight, ran as follows:

"Hillcrest, June 29, 1875.

"Dear Friend Helen:—Something has happened and I am very happy, but I am more than a little troubled over it, too, and, as you are one of the persons nearly concerned, I am going to confess to you as soon as possible. Harry—your brother, I mean—will be sure to tell you very soon, if he hasn't done so already, and I want to make all possible haste to solemnly assure you that I hadn't the slightest idea of such a thing coming to pass, and I didn't do the slightest thing to bring it about.

"I always thought your brother was a splendid fellow, and have never been afraid to express my mind about him, when there was no one but girls to listen. But out here, I have somehow learned to admire him more than ever. I cheerfully acquit him of intentionally doing anything to create a favorable impression; if his several appearances before me have been studied, he is certainly the most original being I ever heard of. Your children are angels—you've told me so yourself, and I've my own very distinct impression on the subject, but they don't study to save their uncle's appearance. The figures that unfortunate man has cut several times—well, I won't try to describe them on paper, for fear he might some day see a scrap of it and take offense. But he always seems to be patient with them, and devoted to them, and I haven't been able to keep from seeing that a man who could be so lovable with thoughtless and unreasonable children must be perfectly adorable to the woman he loved, if she were a woman at all. Still, I hadn't the faintest idea that I would be the fortunate woman. At last the day came, but I was in blissful ignorance of what was to happen. Your little Charley hurt himself, and insisted upon Har—your brother singing an odd song to him; and just when the young gentleman was doing the elegant to a dozen of us ladies at once, too! If you could have seen his face!—it was too funny, until he got over his annoyance, and began to feel properly sorry for the little fellow—then he seemed all at once to be all tenderness and heart, and I did wish for a moment that conventionalities didn't exist, and I might tell him that he was a model. Then your youngest playfully spilt a plate of soup on my dress (don't be worried— 'twas only a common muslin, and 'twill wash). Of course I had to change it and, as I retired, the happy thought struck me that I'd make so elaborate a toilet that I wouldn't finish in time to join the other ladies for the usual evening walk; consequence, I would have a chance to monopolize a gentleman for half an hour or more—a chance which, no thanks to the gentlemen who don't come to Hillcrest, no lady here has had this season. Every time I peered through the blinds to see if the other girls had started, I could see him looking so distressed, and brooding over those two children as if he were their mother, and he seemed so good. He seemed pleased to see me when I appeared, and coming from such a man the implied compliment was fully appreciated; everything he said to me seemed a little more worth hearing than if it had come from any man not so good. Then, suddenly, your eldest insisted on retailing the result of a conversation he had had with his uncle, and the upshot was that Harry declared himself; he wasn't romantic a bit, but he was real straightforward and manly, while I was so completely taken back that I couldn't think of a thing to say. Then the impudent fellow kissed me, and I lost my tongue worse than ever. If I had known anything of his feelings beforehand, I should have been prepared to behave more properly; but—O Helen, I'm so glad I didn't know! I should be the happiest being that ever lived, if I wasn't afraid that you or your husband might think that I had given myself away too hastily. As to other people, we will see that they don't know a word about it for months to come.

"Do write that I was not to blame, and make believe accept me as a sister, because I can't offer to give Harry up to any one else you may have picked out for him.

"Your sincere friend,

"Alice Mayton."

I SHOUTED "HURRAH".

Was there ever so delightful a reveille? All the boyishness in me seemed suddenly to come to the surface, and instead of saying and doing the decorous thing which novelists' heroes do under similar circumstances. I shouted "Hurrah!" and danced into the children's room so violently that Budge sat up in bed and regarded me with reproving eyes, while Toddie burst into a happy laugh, and volunteered as a partner in the dance. Then I realized that the rain was over, and the sun was shining—I could take Alice out for another drive, and until then the children could take care of themselves. I remembered suddenly, and with a sharp pang, that my vacation was nearly at an end, and I found myself consuming with impatience to know how much longer Alice would remain at Hillcrest. It would be cruel to wish her in the city before the end of August, yet I——

"Uncle Harry," said Budge, "my papa says 'tisn't nice for folks to sit down an' go to thinkin' before they've brushed their hair mornin's—that's what he tells me."

"I beg your pardon, Budge," said I, springing up in some confusion; "I was thinking over a matter of a great deal of importance."

"What was it—my goat?"

"No—of course not. Don't be silly, Budge."

"Well, I think about him a good deal, an' I don't think it's silly a bit. I hope he'll go to heaven when he dies. Do angels have goat-carriages, Uncle Harry?"

"No, old fellow—they can go about without carriages."

"When I goesh to hebben," said Toddie, rising in bed, "Izhe goin' to have lots of goat cawidjes an' Izhe goin' to tate all ze andjels a-widen."

With many other bits of prophesy and celestial description I was regaled as I completed my toilet, and I hurried out of doors for an opportunity to think without disturbance. Strolling past the hen-yard, I saw a meditative turtle, and, picking him up and

68

shouting to my nephews, I held the reptile up for their inspection. Their window blinds flew open and a unanimous though not exactly harmonious "Oh!" greeted my prize."

"Where did you get it, Uncle Harry?" asked Budge.

"Down by the hen-coop."

Budge's eyes opened wide; he seemed to devote a moment to profound thought, and then he exclaimed:—

"Why, I don't see how the hens could lay such a big thing—just put him in your hat till I come down, will you?"

I dropped the turtle into Budge's wheelbarrow, and made a tour of the flower-borders. The flowers, always full of suggestion to me, seemed suddenly to have new charms and powers; they actually impelled me to try to make rhymes,—me, a steady white-goods salesman! The impulse was too strong to be resisted, though I must admit that the results were pitifully meager:—

"As radiant as that matchless rose
Which poet-artists fancy;
As fair as whitest lily-blows,
As modest as the pansy;
As pure as dew which hides within
Aurora's sun-kissed chalice;
As tender as the primrose sweet—
All this, and more, is Alice."

In inflicting this fragment upon the reader I have not the faintest idea that he can discover any merit in it; I quote it only that a subsequent experience of mine may be more intelligible. When I had composed these wretched lines I became conscious that I had neither pencil nor paper wherewith to preserve them. Should I lose them—my first self-constructed poem? Never! This was not the first time in which I had found it necessary to preserve words by memory alone. So I repeated my ridiculous lines over and over again, until the eloquent feeling of which they were the graceless expression inspired me to accompany my recital with gestures. Six—eight—ten—a dozen—twenty times I repeated these lines, each time with additional emotion and gesture, when a thin voice, very near me, remarked:—

"Ocken Hawwy, you does djust as if you was swimmin'."

Turning, I beheld my nephew, Toddie—how long he had been behind me I had no idea. He looked earnestly into my eyes, and then remarked:—

"Ocken Hawwy, your faysh is wed, djust like a wosy-posy."

"Let's go right in to breakfast, Toddie," said I aloud, as I grumbled to myself about the faculty of observation which Tom's children seemed to have.

Immediately after breakfast I despatched Mike with a note to Alice, informing her that I would be glad to drive her to the Falls in the afternoon, calling for her at two. Then I placed myself unreservedly at the disposal of the boys for the morning, it being distinctly understood that they must not expect to see me between lunch and dinner. I was first instructed to harness the goat, which order I obeyed, and I afterward watched that grave animal as he drew my nephews up and down the carriage-road, his countenance as demure as if he had no idea of suddenly departing when my back should be turned. The wheels of the goat-carriage uttered the most heart-rending noises I had ever heard from ungreased axle; so I persuaded the boys to dismount, and submit to the temporary unharnessing of the goat, while I should lubricate the axles. Half an hour of dirty work sufficed, with such assistance as I gained from juvenile advice, to accomplish the task properly; then I put the horned steed into the shafts, Budge cracked the whip, the carriage moved off without noise, and Toddie began to weep bitterly.

"Cawwidge is all bwoke," said he; "wheelsh don't sing a bittie no more," while Budge remarked:—

"I think the carriage sounds kind o' lonesome now, don't you, Uncle Harry?"

"Uncle Harry," asked Budge, a little later in the morning, "do you know what makes the thunder?"

"Yes, Budge—when two clouds go bump into each other they make a good deal of noise, and they call it thunder."

"That ain't it at all," said Budge "When it thundered yesterday it was because the Lord was riding along through the sky an' the wheels of his carriage made an awful noise, an' that was the thunder."

"Don't like nashty old funder," remarked Toddie. "It goesh into our cellar an' makesh all ze milk sour—Maggie said so. An' so I can't hazh no nice white tea for my brepspup."

"I should think you'd like the Lord to go a-ridin', Toddie, with all the angels running after Him," said Budge, "even if the thunder does make the milk sour. And it's so splendid to see the thunder bang."

"How do you see it, Budge?" I asked.

"Why, don't you know when the thunder bangs, and then you see an awful bright place in the sky?—that's where the Lord's carriage gives an awful pound, an' makes little cracks through the floor of heaven, an' we see right in. But what's the reason we can't ever see anybody through the cracks, Uncle Harry?"

"I don't know, old fellow—I guess it's because it isn't cracks in heaven that look so bright,—it's a kind of fire that the Lord makes up in the clouds. You'll know all about it when you get bigger."

70

"Well, I'll feel awful sorry if 'tain't anything but fire. Do you know that funny song my papa sings 'bout:—

"'Roarin' thunders, lightenin's blazes,
Shout the great Creator's praises?'
I don't know 'zactly what it means, but I think it's kind o' splendid, don't you?"

"TWO CLOUDS GO BUMP INTO EACH OTHER"
I did know the old song; I had heard it in a Western camp-meeting, when scarcely older than Budge, and it left upon my mind just the effect it seemed to have done on his. I blessed his sympathetic young heart, and snatched him into my arms. Instantly, he became all boy again.

"Uncle Harry," he shouted, "you crawl on your hands and knees and play you was a horse, and I'll ride on your back."

"No, thank you, Budge, not on the dirt."

"Then let's play menagerie, an' you be all the animals."

To this proposition I assented, and after hiding ourselves in one of the retired angles of the house, so that no one could know who was guilty of disturbing the peace by such dire noises, the performance commenced. I was by turns a bear, a lion, a zebra, an elephant, dogs of various kinds, and a cat. As I personated the latter named animal, Toddie echoed my voice.

"Miauw! Miauw!" said he, "dat's what cats saysh when they goesh down wells."

"Faith, an' it's him that knows," remarked Mike, who had invited himself to a free seat in the menagerie, and assisted in the applause which had greeted each personation. "Would ye belave it, Misther Harry, dhat young dhivil got out the front door one mornin' afore sunroise, all in his little noight-gown, an' wint over to dhe docthor's an' picked up a kitten lyin' on dhe kitchen door-mat, an' throwed it down dhe well. Dhe docthor wasn't home, but dhe missis saw him, an' her heart was dhat tindher dhat she hurried out and throwed boords down for dhe poor little baste to stand on, an' let down a hoe on a sthring, an' whin she got dhe poor little dhing out, she was dhat faint dhat she dhrapped on dhe grass. An' it cost Mr. Lawrence nigh onto thirty dollars to have the docthor's well claned out."

"Yes," said Toddie, who had listened carefully to Mike's recital, "An' kitty-kitty said, 'Miauw! Miauw!' when she goed down ze well. An' Mish Doctor sed, 'Bad boy—go home—don't never turn to my housh no more,'—dat's what she said to me. Now be some more animals, Ocken Hawwy. Can't you be a whay-al?"

"Whales don't make a noise, Toddie; they only splash about in the water."

"Zen grop in ze cistern an' 'plash, can't you?"

71

Lunch-time, and after it the time for Toddie to take his nap. Poor Budge was bereft of a playmate, for the doctor's little girl was sick; so he quietly followed me about with a wistful face, that almost persuaded me to take him with me on my drive—our drive. Had he grumbled, I would have felt less uncomfortable; but there's nothing so touching and overpowering to either gods or men, as the spectacle of mute resignation. At last, to my great relief, he opened his mouth.

"Uncle Harry," said he, "do you s'pose folks ever get lonesome in heaven?"

"I guess not, Budge."

"Do little boy angels' papas an' mammas go off visitin', an' stay ever so long?"

"I don't exactly know, Budge, but if they do, the little boy angels have plenty of other little boy angels to play with, so they can't very well be lonesome."

"Well, I don't b'leeve they could make me happy, when I wanted to see my papa an' mamma. When I haven't got anybody to play with, then I want papa an' mamma so bad—so bad as if I would die if I didn't see 'em right away."

"CAN'T YOU BE A WHAY-AL?"
I was shaving, and only half-done, but I hastily wiped off my face, dropped into a rocking-chair, took the forlorn little boy into my arms, and kissed him, caressed him, sympathized with him, and devoted myself entirely to the task and pleasure of comforting him. His sober little face gradually assumed a happier appearance; his lips parted in such lines as no old master ever put upon angel lips; his eyes, from being dim and hopeless, grew warm and lustrous and melting. At last he said:—

"Uncle Harry, I'm ever so happy now. An' can't Mike go around with me and the goat, all the time you're away riding? An bring us home some candy, an' marbles—oh, yes—an' a new dog."

Anxious as I was to hurry off to meet my engagement, I was rather disgusted as I unseated Budge and returned to my razor. So long as he was lonesome and I was his only hope, words couldn't express his devotion, but the moment he had, through my efforts, regained his spirits, his only use for me was to ask further favors. Yet in trying the poor boy, judicially, the evidence was more dangerous to humanity in general than to Budge; it threw a great deal of light upon my own peculiar theological puzzles, and almost convinced me that my duty was to preach a new gospel.

As I drove up to the steps of Mrs. Clarkson's boarding-house, it seemed to me a month had elapsed since last I was there, and this apparent lapse of time was all that prevented my ascribing to miraculous agencies the wonderful and delightful change that Alice's countenance had undergone in two short days. Composure, quickness of perception, the ability to guard one's self, are indications of character which are particularly in place in the countenance of a young lady in society, but when, without losing these, the face takes on the radiance born of love and trust, the effect is indescribably charming—especially to the eyes of the man who causes the change. Longer, more out-of-the-way roads between Hillcrest and the Falls, I venture to say, were never known than I drove over that afternoon, and my happy companion, who in other days I had imagined might one day, by her decision, alertness and force exceed the exploits of Lady Baker, or Miss Tinne, never once asked if I was sure we were on the right road. Only a single cloud came over her brow, and of this I soon learned the cause.

"Harry," said she, pressing closer to my side, and taking an appealing tone, "do you love me well enough to endure something unpleasant for my sake?"

My answer was not verbally expressed, but its purport seemed to be understood and accepted, for Alice continued:—

"I wouldn't undo a bit of what's happened—I'm the happiest, proudest woman in the world. But we have been very hasty, for people who have been mere acquaintances. And mother is dreadfully opposed to such affairs—she is of the old style, you know."

"It was all my fault," said I. "I'll apologize promptly and handsomely. The time and agony which I didn't consume in laying siege to your heart, I'll devote to the task of gaining your mother's good graces."

The look I received in reply to this remark would have richly repaid me, had my task been to conciliate as many mothers-in-law as Brigham Young possesses. But her smile faded as she said:—

"You don't know what a task you have before you. Mother has a very tender heart, but it's thoroughly fenced in by proprieties. In her day and set, courtship was a very slow, stately affair, and mother believes it the proper way now; so do I, but I admit possible exceptions, and mother does not. I am afraid she won't be patient if she knows the whole truth, yet I can't bear to keep it from her. I'm her only child, you know."

"Don't keep it from her," said I, "unless for some reason of your own. Let me tell the whole story, take all the responsibility, and accept the penalties, if there are any. Your mother is right in principle, if there is a certain delightful exception that we know of."

"My only fear is for you," said my darling, nestling closer to me. "She comes of a family that can display most glorious indignation when there's a good excuse for it, and I can't bear to think of you being the cause of such an outbreak."

"I've faced the ugliest of guns in honor of one form of love, little girl," I replied, "and I could do even more for the sentiment for which you're to blame. And for my own sake, I'd rather endure anything than a sense of having deceived any one, especially the mother of such a daughter. Besides, you're her dearest treasure, and she has a right to know of even the least thing that in any way concerns you."

"And you're a noble fellow, and——" Whatever other sentiment my companion failed to put into words was impulsively and eloquently communicated by her dear eyes.

73

But oh, what a cowardly heart your dear cheek rested upon an instant later, fair Alice! Not for the first time in my life did I shrink and tremble at the realization of what duty imperatively required—not for the first time did I go through a harder battle than was ever fought with sword and cannon, and a battle with greater possibilities of danger than the field ever offered. I won it, as a man must do in such fights, if he deserves to live; but I could not help feeling considerably sobered on our homeward drive.

We neared the house, and I had an insane fancy that instead of driving two horses I was astride of one, with spurs at my heels and a saber at my side.

"Let me talk to her now, Alice, won't you? Delays are only cowardly."

A slight trembling at my side—an instant of silence that seemed an hour, yet within which I could count but six footfalls, and Alice replied:—

"Yes; if the parlor happens to be empty, I'll ask her if she won't go in and see you a moment." Then there came a look full of tenderness, wonder, painful solicitude, and then two dear eyes filled with tears.

"We're nearly there, darling," said I, with a reassuring embrace.

"Yes, and you sha'n't be the only hero," said she, straightening herself proudly, and looking a fit model for a Zenobia.

As we passed from behind a clump of evergreens which hid the house from our view, I involuntarily exclaimed, "Gracious!" Upon the piazza stood Mrs. Mayton; at her side stood my two nephews, as dirty in face, in clothing, as I had ever seen them. I don't know but that for a moment I freely forgave them, for their presence might grant me the respite which a sense of duty would not allow me to take.

"Wezhe comed up to wide home wif you," exclaimed Toddie, as Mrs. Mayton greeted me with an odd mixture of courtesy, curiosity and humor. Alice led the way into the parlor, whispered to her mother, and commenced to make a rapid exit, when Mrs. Mayton called her back, and motioned her to a chair. Alice and I exchanged sidelong glances.

"Alice says you wish to speak with me, Mr. Burton," said she. "I wonder whether the subject is one upon which I have this afternoon received a minute verbal account from the elder Master Lawrence."

Alice looked blank;—I am sure that I did. But safety could only lie in action, so I stammered out:——

"If you refer to an apparently unwarrantable intrusion upon your family circle, Mrs.——"

"I do, sir," replied the old lady. "Between the statements made by that child, and the hitherto unaccountable change in my daughter's looks during two or three days, I think I have got at the truth of the matter. If the offender was any one else, I should be inclined to be severe; but we mothers of only daughters are apt to have a pretty distinct idea of the merits of young men, and——"

The old lady dropped her head; I sprang to my feet, seized her hand, and reverently kissed it; then Mrs. Mayton, whose only son had died fifteen years before, raised her head and adopted me in the manner peculiar to mothers, while Alice burst into tears, and kissed us both.

A few moments later, as three happy people were occupying conventional attitudes, and trying to compose faces which should bear the inspection of whoever might happen into the parlor, Mrs. Mayton observed:—

"My children, between us this matter is understood, but I must caution you against acting in such a way as to make the engagement public at once."

"Trust me for that," hastily exclaimed Alice.

"And me," said I.

"I have no doubt of the intention and discretion of either of you," resumed Mrs. Mayton, "but you cannot possibly be too cautious." Here a loud laugh from the shrubbery under the windows drowned Mrs. Mayton's voice for a moment, but she continued: "Servants, children,"—here she smiled, and I dropped my head—"persons you may chance to meet——"

Again the laugh broke forth under the window.

"What can those girls be laughing at?" exclaimed Alice, moving toward the window, followed by her mother and me.

Seated in a semicircle on the grass were most of the ladies boarding at Mrs. Clarkson's, and in front of them stood Toddie, in that high state of excitement to which sympathetic applause always raises him.

"Say it again," said one of the ladies.

Toddie put on an expression of profound wisdom, made violent gestures with both hands, and repeated the following, with frequent gesticulations:—

"Azh wadiant azh ze matchless woze
Zat poeck-artuss fanshy;
Azh fair azh whituss lily-blowzh;
Azh moduss azh a panzhy;
Azh pure azh dew zat hides wiffin
Awwahwah's sun-tissed tsallish;
Azh tender azh ze pwimwose tweet,
All zish, an' moah, izh Alish."

"AZH WADIANT AZH ZE MATCHLESS WOZE"
I gasped for breath.

"Who taught you all that, Toddie?" asked one of the ladies.

"Nobody didn't taught me—I lyned[9] it."

[9] Learned.

"When did you learn it?"

"Lyned it zish mornin'. Ocken Hawwy said it over, an' over, an' over, djust yots of timezh, out in ze garden."

The ladies all exchanged glances—my lady readers will understand just how, and I assure gentlemen that I did not find their glances at all hard to read. Alice looked at me inquiringly, and she now tells me that I blushed sheepishly and guiltily. Poor Mrs. Mayton staggered to a chair, and exclaimed:

"Too late! too late!"

Considering their recent achievements, Toddie and Budge were a very modest couple as I drove them home that evening. Budge even made some attempt at apologizing for their appearance, saying that they couldn't find Maggie, and couldn't wait any longer; but I assured him that no apology was necessary. I was in such excellent spirits that my feeling became contagious; and we sang songs, told stories, and played ridiculous games most of the evening, paying but little attention to the dinner that was set for us.

"Uncle Harry," said Budge, suddenly, "do you know we haven't ever sung,—

'Drown old Pharaoh's Army, Hallelujah,'
since you've been here? Let's do it now."

"All right, old fellow." I knew the song—such as there was of it—and its chorus, as every one does who ever heard the Jubilee Singers render it; but I scarcely understood the meaning of the preparations which Budge made. He drew a large rocking-chair into the middle of the room, and exclaimed:—

"There, Uncle Harry—you sit down. Come along, Tod—you sit on that knee, and I'll sit on this. Lift up both hands, Tod, like I do. Now we're all ready, Uncle Harry."

I sang the first line:—

"When Israel was in bondage, they cried unto the Lord,"
without any assistance, but the boys came in powerfully on the refrain, beating time simultaneously with their four fists upon my chest. I cannot think it strange that I suddenly ceased singing, but the boys viewed my action from a different standpoint.

"What makes you stop, Uncle Harry?" asked Budge.

"Because you hurt me badly, my boy; you mustn't do that again."

"Why, I guess you ain't very strong: that's the way we do to papa, an' it don't hurt him."

Poor Tom! No wonder he grows flat-chested.

"Guesh you's a ky-baby," suggested Toddie.

This imputation I bore with meekness, but ventured to remark that it was bedtime. After allowing a few moments for the usual expressions of dissent, I staggered upstairs with Toddie in my arms, and Budge on my back, both boys roaring the refrain of the negro hymn:—

"I'm a-rolling through an unfriendly World!"
The offer of a stick of candy to whichever boy was first undressed, caused some lively disrobing, after which each boy received the prize. Budge bit a large piece, wedged it between his cheek and his teeth, closed his eyes, folded his hands on his breast, and prayed:—

"Dear Lord, bless papa an' mamma, an' Toddie an' me, an' that turtle Uncle Harry found; and bless that lovely lady Uncle Harry goes ridin' with, an' make 'em take me too, an' bless that nice old lady with white hair, that cried, an' said I was a smart boy. Amen."

Toddie sighed as he drew his stick of candy from his lips; then he shut his eyes and remarked:—"Dee Lord, blesh Toddie, an' make him good boy, an' blesh zem ladies zat told me to say it aden"; the particular "it" referred to being well understood by at least three adults of my acquaintance.

The course of Budge's interview with Mrs. Mayton was afterward related by that lady, as follows:—

She was sitting in her own room (which was on the parlor floor, and in the rear of the house), and was leisurely reading "Fated to be Free," when she accidentally dropped her glasses. Stooping to pick them up, she became aware that she was not alone. A small, very dirty, but good-featured boy stood before her, his hands behind his back, and an inquiring look in his eyes.

"Run away, little boy," said she. "Don't you know it isn't polite to enter rooms without knocking?"

"I'm lookin' for my uncle," said Budge, in most melodious accents, "an' the other ladies said you would know when he would come back."

"I'm afraid they were making fun of you—or me," said the old lady, a little severely. "I don't know anything about little boys' uncles. Now, run away, and don't disturb me any more."

"Well," continued Budge, "they said your little girl went with him, and you'd know when she would come back."

"I haven't any little girl," said the old lady, her indignation at a supposed joke threatening to overcome her dignity. "Now go away."

"She isn't a very little girl," said Budge, honestly anxious to conciliate; "that is, she's bigger'n I am, but they said you was her mother, an' so she's your little girl, isn't she? I think she's lovely, too."

MRS. MAYTON STOOPED TO PICK UP HER GLASSES
"Do you mean Miss Mayton?" asked the lady, thinking she had a possible clue to the cause of Budge's anxiety.

"Oh, yes—that's her name—I couldn't think of it," eagerly replied Budge. "An ain't she AWFUL nice—I know she is!"

"Your judgment is quite correct, considering your age," said Mrs. Mayton, exhibiting more interest in Budge than she had heretofore done. "But what makes you think she is nice? You are rather younger than her male admirers usually are."

"Why, my Uncle Harry told me so," replied Budge, "and he knows everything."

Mrs. Mayton grew vigilant at once, and dropped her book.

"Who is your Uncle Harry, little boy?"

"He's Uncle Harry; don't you know him? He can make nicer whistles than my papa can. An' he found a turtle——"

"Who is your papa?" interrupted the old lady.

"Why, he's papa—I thought everybody knew who he was."

"What is your name?" asked Mrs. Mayton.

"John Burton Lawrence," promptly answered Budge.

Mrs. Mayton wrinkled her brows for a moment, and finally asked:—

"Is Mr. Burton the uncle you are looking for?"

"I don't know any Mr. Burton," said Budge, a little dazed; "uncle is mamma's brother, an' he's been livin' at our house ever since mamma and papa went off visitin', an' he goes ridin' in our carriage, an'——"

"Humph!" remarked the old lady with so much emphasis that Budge ceased talking. A moment later she said:—

"I didn't mean to interrupt you, little boy; go on."

"An' he rides with just the loveliest lady that ever was. He thinks so, an' I KNOW she is. An' he 'spects her."

"What?" exclaimed the old lady.

"'Spects her, I say—that's what he says. I say 'spect means just what I call love. 'Cos if it don't, what makes him give her hugs an' kisses?"

Mrs. Mayton caught her breath—and did not reply for a moment. At last she said:—

"How do you know he—gives her hugs and kisses?"

"'Cos I saw him, the day Toddie hurt his finger in the grass cutter. An' he was so happy that he bought me a goat-carriage next morning—I'll show it to you if you come down to our stable, an' I'll show you the goat too. An' he bought——"

Just here Budge stopped, for Mrs. Mayton put her handkerchief to her eyes. Two or three moments later she felt a light touch on her knee, and, wiping her eyes, saw Budge looking sympathetically into her face.

"I'm awful sorry you feel bad," said he. "Are you 'fraid to have your little girl ridin' so long?"

"Yes!" exclaimed Mrs. Mayton, with great decision.

"Well, you needn't be," said Budge, "for Uncle Harry's awful careful an' smart."

"He ought to be ashamed of himself!" exclaimed the lady.

"I guess he is, then," said Budge, "'cos he's ev'rything he ought to be. He's awful careful. T'other day, when the goat ran away, an' Toddie an' me got in the carriage with them, he held on to her tight, so she couldn't fall out."

Mrs. Mayton brought her foot down with a violent stamp.

"I know you'd 'spect him, if you knew how nice he was," continued Budge. "He sings awful funny songs, an' tells splendid stories."

"Nonsense!" exclaimed the angry mother.

"They ain't no nonsense at all," said Budge. "I don't think it's nice for to say that, when his stories are always about Joseph, an' Abraham, an' Moses, an' when Jesus was a little boy, an' the Hebrew children, an' lots of people that the Lord loved. An' he's awful 'fectionate, too."

"Yes, I suppose so," said Mrs. Mayton.

"When we says our prayers we prays for the nice lady what he 'spects, an' he likes us to do it," continued Budge.

"How do you know?" demanded Mrs. Mayton.

"'Cos he always kisses us when we do it an' that's what my papa does when he likes what we pray."

Mrs. Mayton's mind became absorbed in earnest thought, but Budge had not said all that was in his heart.

"An' when Toddie or me tumbles down an hurts ourselves, 'tain't no matter what Uncle Harry's doin', he runs right out an' picks us up an' comforts us. He froed away a cigar the other day, he was in such a hurry when a wasp stung me, an' Toddie picked the cigar up and ate it, an' it made him awful sick."

The last-named incident did not affect Mrs. Mayton deeply, perhaps on the score of inapplicability to the question before her. Budge went on:—

"An' wasn't he good to me to-day? Just 'cos I was forlorn, 'cos I hadn't nobody to play with, an' wanted to die an' go to heaven, he stopped shavin', so as to comfort me."

Mrs. Mayton had been thinking rapidly and seriously, and her heart had relented somewhat toward the principal offender.

"Suppose," she said, "that I don't let my little girl go riding with him any more?"

MADE HIM AWFUL SICK
"Then," said Budge, "I know he'll be awful, awful unhappy, an' I'll be awful sorry for him, 'cos nice folks oughtn't to be made unhappy."

"Suppose, then, that I do let her go?" said Mrs. Mayton.

"Then I'll give you a whole stomachful of kisses for being so good to my uncle," said Budge. And assuming that the latter course would be the one adopted by Mrs. Mayton, Budge climbed into her lap and began at once to make payment.

"Bless your dear little heart! exclaimed Mrs. Mayton; "you're of the same blood, and it is good, if it is rather hasty."

As I rose the next morning, I found a letter under my door. Disappointed that it was not addressed in Alice's writing, I was nevertheless glad to get a word from my sister, particularly as the letter ran as follows:—

"July 1, 1875.

"Dear Old Brother:—I've been recalling a fortnight's experience we once had of courtship in a boarding-house, and I've determined to cut short our visit here, hurry home, and give you and Alice a chance or two to see each other in parlors where there won't be a likelihood of the dozen or two interruptions you must suffer each evening now. Tom agrees with me, like the obedient old darling that he is; so please have the carriage at Hillcrest station for us at 11:40 Friday morning. Invite Alice and her mother for me to dine with us Sunday,—we'll bring them home from church with us.

"Lovingly your sister,
"Helen.
"P. S. Of course you'll have my darlings in the carriage to receive me.

"P. S. Would it annoy you to move into the best guest-chamber? I can't bear to sleep where I can't have them within reach."

Friday morning they intended to arrive,—blessings on their thoughtful hearts!—and this was Friday. I hurried into the boys' room and shouted:—

"Toddie! Budge! who do you think is coming to see you this morning?"

"Who?" asked Budge.

"Organ-grinder?" queried Toddie.

"No, your papa and mamma."

Budge looked like an angel in an instant, but Toddie's eyes twitched a little, and he mournfully murmured:—

"I fought it wash an organ-grinder."

"O Uncle Harry!" said Budge, springing out of bed in a perfect delirium of delight, "I believe if my papa and mamma had stayed away any longer, I believe I would die. I've been so lonesome for 'em that I haven't known what to do—I've cried whole pillowsful about it, right here in the dark."

"Why, my poor old fellow," said I, picking him up and kissing him, "why didn't you come up and tell Uncle Harry, and let him try to comfort you?"

"I couldn't," said Budge; "when I gets lonesome, it feels as if my mouth was all tied up, an' a great big stone was right in here." And Budge put his hand on his chest.

"If a big 'tone wazh inshide of me," said Toddie, "I'd take it out an' fro it at the shickens."

"Toddie," said I, "aren't you glad papa and mamma are coming?"

"Yesh," said Toddie, "I fink it'll be awfoo nish. Mamma always bwings me candy fen she goes away anyfere."

"Toddie, you're a mercenary wretch."

"Ain't a mernesary wetch; Izhe Toddie Yawncie."

Toddie made none the less haste in dressing than his brother, however. Candy was to him what some systems of theology are to their adherents—not a very lofty motive of action, but sweet, and something he could fully understand; so the energy displayed in getting himself tangled up in his clothes was something wonderful.

"Stop, boys," said I; "you must have on clean clothes to-day. You don't want your father and mother to see you all dirty, do you?"

"Of course not," said Budge.

"Oh, izh I goin' to be djessed up all nicey?" asked Toddie. "Goody! goody! goody!"

I always thought my sister Helen had an undue amount of vanity, and here it was reappearing in the second generation.

"An' I wantsh my shoes made all nigger," said Toddie.

"What?"

"Wantsh my shoes made all nigger wif a bottle-bwush, too," said Toddie.

I looked appealingly at Budge, who answered:—

"He means he wants his shoes blacked, with the polish that's in the bottle, an' you rub it on with a brush."

"An' I wantsh a thath on," continued Toddie.

"Sash, he means," said Budge. "He's awful proud."

"An' Izhe doin' to wear my takker-hat," said Toddie. "An' my wed djuvs."

"That's his tassel-hat an' his red gloves," continued the interpreter.

"Toddie, you can't wear gloves such hot days as these," said I.

A look of inquiry was speedily followed by Toddie's own unmistakable preparations for weeping; and as I did not want his eyes dimmed when his mother looked into them I hastily exclaimed:—

"Put them on, then—put on the mantle of rude Boreas if you choose; but don't go to crying."

"Don't want no mantle-o'wude-baw-yusses," declared Toddie, following me phonetically, "wantsh my own pitty cozhesh, an' nobody eshesh."

"O Uncle Harry," exclaimed Budge, "I want to bring mamma home in my goat-carriage!"

"The goat isn't strong enough, Budge, to draw mamma and you."

"Well, then, let me drive down to the depot, just to show papa an' mamma I've got a goat-carriage—I'm sure mamma would be very unhappy when she found out I had one, and she hadn't seen it first thing."

"Well, I guess you may follow me down, Budge; but you must drive very carefully."

"Oh, yes—I wouldn't get us hurt when mamma was coming for anything."

"THE SUN'LL BE DISAPPOINTED IF IT DON'T HAVE US TO LOOK AT"
"Now, boys," said I, "I want you to stay in the house and play this morning. If you go out of doors you'll get yourselves dirty."

"I guess the sun'll be disappointed if it don't have us to look at," suggested Budge.

"Never mind," said I, "the sun's old enough to have learned to be patient."

Breakfast over, the boys moved reluctantly away to the play-room, while I inspected the house and grounds pretty closely, to see that everything should at least fail to do my management discredit. A dollar given to Mike and another to Maggie were of material assistance in this work, so I felt free to adorn the parlors and Helen's chamber with flowers. As I went into the latter room I heard some one at the wash-stand, which was in an alcove and, on looking in, I saw Toddie drinking the last of the contents of a goblet which contained a dark-colored mixture.

"Izhe tatin' black medshin," said Toddie; "I likes black medshin awfoo muts."

"What do you make it of?" I asked, with some sympathy, and tracing parental influence again. When Helen and I were children we spent hours in soaking licorice in water and administering it as medicine.

"Makesh it out of shoda mitsture," said Toddie.

This was another medicine of our childhood days, but one prepared according to physician's prescription, and not beneficial when taken ad libitum. As I took the vial—a two-ounce one—I asked:—

"How much did you take, Toddie?"

"Took whole bottoo full—'twas nysh," said he.

Suddenly, the label caught my eye—it read PAREGORIC. In a second I had snatched a shawl, wrapped Toddie in it, tucked him under my arm, and was on my way to the barn. In a moment more I was on one of the horses and galloping furiously to the village, with Toddie under one arm, his yellow curls streaming in the breeze. People came out and stared as they did at John Gilpin, while one old farmer whom I met turned his team about, whipped up furiously, and followed me, shouting, "Stop, thief!" I afterward learned that he took me to be one of the abductors of Charlie Ross, with the lost child under my arm, and that visions of the $20,000 reward floated before his eyes. In front of an apothecary's I brought the horse suddenly upon his haunches, and dashed in, exclaiming:—

"Give this child a strong emetic—quick! He's swallowed poison!"

The apothecary hurried to his prescription-desk, while a motherly-looking Irish woman upon whom he had been waiting, exclaimed, "Holy Mither! I'll run an' fetch Father O'Kelley," and hurried out. Meanwhile Toddie, upon whom the medicine had not commenced to take effect, had seized the apothecary's cat by the tail, which operation resulted in a considerable vocal protest from that animal.

The experiences of the next few moments were more pronounced and revolutionary than pleasing to relate in detail. It is sufficient to say that Toddie's weight was materially diminished, and that his complexion was temporarily pallid. Father O'Kelley arrived at a brisk run, and was honestly glad to find that his services were not required, although I assured him that if Catholic baptism and a sprinkling of holy water would have improved Toddie's character, I thought there was excuse for several applications. We rode quietly back to the house, and while I was asking Maggie to try and coax Toddie into taking a nap, I heard the patient remark to his brother:—

GALLOPING FURIOUSLY TO THE VILLAGE
"Budgie, down to the village I was a whay-al. I didn't froe up Djonah, but I froed up a whole floor full of uvver fings."

During the hour which passed before it was time to start for the depot my sole attention was devoted to keeping the children from soiling their clothes; but my success was so little, that I lost my temper entirely. First they insisted upon playing on a part of the lawn which the sun had not yet reached. Then, while I had gone into the house for a match to light my cigar, Toddie had gone with his damp shoes into the middle of the road, where the dust was ankle deep. Then they got upon their hands and knees on the piazza and played bear. Each one wanted to pick a bouquet for his mother, and Toddie took the precaution to smell every flower he approached—an operation which caused him to get his nose covered with lily-pollen, so that he looked like a badly used prize-fighter. In one of their spasms of inaction, Budge asked:—

"What makes some of the men in church have no hair on the tops of their heads, Uncle Harry?"

"Because," said I, pausing long enough to shake Toddie for trying to get my watch out of my pocket, "because they have bad little boys to bother them all the time, so their hair drops out."

"I dess my hairs is a-goin' to drop out pitty soon, then," remarked Toddie, with an injured air.

MIKE TELLING MAGGIE TO GET LUNCH
"Harness the horses, Mike!" I shouted.

"An' the goat, too," added Budge.

Five minutes later I was seated in the carriage, or rather in Tom's two-seated open wagon. "Mike," I shouted, "I forgot to tell Maggie to have some lunch ready for the folks when they get here—run, tell her, quick, won't you?"

"Oye, oye, sur," said Mike, and off he went.

"Are you all ready, boys?" I asked.

"In a minute," said Budge; "soon as I fix this. Now," he continued, getting into his seat, and taking the reins and whip, "go ahead."

"Wait a moment, Budge—put down that whip, and don't touch the goat with it once on the way. I'm going to drive very slowly—there's plenty of time, and all you need to do is to hold your reins."

"All right," said Budge, "but I like to look like mans when I drive."

"You may do that when somebody can run beside you. Now!"

The horses started at a gentle trot, and the goat followed very closely. When within a minute of the depot, however, the train swept in. I had intended to be on the platform to meet Tom and Helen, but my watch was evidently slow. I gave the horses the whip, looked behind and saw the boys were close upon me, and I was so near the platform when I turned my head that nothing but the sharpest of turns saved me from a severe accident. The noble animals saw the danger as quickly as I did, however, and turned in marvelously small space; as they did so, I heard two hard thumps upon the wooden wall of the little depot, heard also two frightful howls, saw both my nephews considerably mixed up on the platform, while the driver of the Bloom-Park stage growled in my ear:—

85

"What in thunder did you let 'em hitch that goat to your axle-tree for?"

I looked, and saw the man spoke with just cause. How the goat's head and shoulders had maintained their normal connection during the last minute of my drive, I leave for naturalists to explain. I had no time to meditate on the matter just then, for the train had stopped. Fortunately the children had struck on their heads, and the Lawrence-Burton skull is a marvel of solidity. I set them upon their feet, brushed them off with my hands, promised them all the candy they could eat for a week, wiped their eyes, and hurried them to the other side of the depot. Budge rushed at Tom, exclaiming:—

"See my goat, papa!"

Helen opened her arms, and Toddie threw himself into them, sobbing:—

"Mam—ma! shing 'Toddie one-boy-day!'"

How uncomfortable a man can feel in the society of a dearly beloved sister and an incomparable brother-in-law I never imagined until that short drive. Helen was somewhat concerned about the children, but she found time to look at me with so much of sympathy, humor, affection, and condescension that I really felt relieved when we reached the house. I hastily retired to my own room, but before I had shut the door Helen was with me, and her arms were about my neck; before the dear old girl removed them we had grown far nearer to each other than we had ever been before.

And how gloriously the rest of the day passed off. We had a delightful little lunch, and Tom brought up a bottle of Roederer, and Helen didn't remonstrate when he insisted on its being drank from her finest glasses, and there were toasts drank to "Her" and "Her Mother," and to the Benedict that was to be. And then Helen proposed "The makers of the match—Budge and Toddie!" which was honored with bumpers. The gentlemen toasted did not respond, but they stared so curiously that I sprang from my chair and kissed them soundly, upon which Tom and Helen exchanged significant glances.

Then Helen walked down to Mrs. Clarkson's boarding-house, all for the purpose of showing a lady there, with a skirt to make over, just how she had seen a similar garment rearranged exquisitely. And Alice strolled down to the gate with her to say good-by; and they had so much to talk about that Helen walked Alice nearly to our house, and then insisted on her coming the rest of the way, so she might be driven home. And then Mike was sent back with a note to say to Mrs. Mayton that her daughter had been prevailed upon to stay to evening dinner, but would be sent home under capable escort. And after dinner was over and the children put to bed, Tom groaned that he must attend a road-board meeting, and Helen begged us to excuse her just a minute while she ran in to the doctor's to ask how poor Mrs. Brown had been doing, and she consumed three hours and twenty-five minutes in asking, bless her sympathetic soul!

The dreaded ending of my vacation did not cause me as many pangs as I had expected. Helen wanted to know one evening why if her poor, dear Tom could go back and forth to the city to business every day, her lazy big brother couldn't go back and forth to Hillcrest daily, if she were to want him as a boarder for the remainder of the season. Although I had for years inveighed against the folly of cultivated people leaving the city to find residences, Helen's argument was unanswerable and I submitted. I did even more; I purchased a lovely bit of ground (though the deed stands in Tom's name for the present), and Tom has brought up several plans for cottage-houses, and every evening they are spread on the dining-room table, and there gather round them four people, among whom are a white goods salesman and a young lady with the brightest of eyes and cheeks full of roses and lilies. This latter-named personage has her own opinions of the merits of all plans suggested, and insisted that whatever plan is adopted must have a lovely room to be set apart as the exclusive property of Helen's boys. Young as these gentlemen are, I find frequent occasions to be frightfully jealous of them, but they are unmoved by either my frowns or persuasions—artifice alone is able to prevent their monopolizing the time of an adorable being, of whose society I cannot possibly have too much. She insists that when the ceremony takes place in December, they shall officiate as groomsmen, and I have not the slightest doubt that she will carry her point. In fact, I confess to frequent affectionate advances toward them myself, and when I retire without first seeking their room and putting a grateful kiss upon their unconscious lips, my conscience upbraids me with base ingratitude. To think I might yet be a hopeless bachelor had it not been for them, is to overflow with thankfulness to the giver of

Helen's Babies.

Printed in Great Britain
by Amazon

53607056R00052